Adventures in Jamestown

Liberty Letters®

Adventures in Jamestown

Nancy LeSourd

ZONDERVAN.com/
AUTHORTRACKER
follow your favorite authors

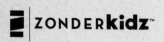

ZONDER**kidz**™

www.zonderkidz.com

Adventures in Jamestown

Previously published as *The Personal Correspondence of Elizabeth Walton and Abigail Matthews*
Copyright © 2003, 2008 by Nancy Oliver LeSourd

Requests for information should be addressed to:
Zonderkidz, Grand Rapids, Michigan 49530

Library of Congress Cataloging-in-Publication Data

LeSourd, Nancy.
      Adventures in Jamestown / by Nancy LeSourd.
        p. cm. --(Liberty letters)
   Previously published in slightly altered form as: The personal correspondence of Elizabeth
Walton and Abigail Matthews. 2003
   Summary: Letters between two young girls, one in London and the other in English settlements
in Virginia, chronicle the events during the difficult early years at James Towne and Henricus
and the role of Pocahontas in this period of history
      ISBN 978-0-310-71392-0 (softcover)
   1. Jamestown (Va.)--History--Juvenile fiction. 2. Pocahontas, d. 1617--Juvenile fiction. [1.
Jamestown (Va.)--History--Fiction. 2. Pocahontas, d. 1617--Fiction. 3. Virginia--History--Colonial
period, ca. 1600-1775--Fiction. 4. Christian life--Fiction. 5. Letters--Fiction.] I. LeSourd, Nancy.
Personal correspondence of Elizabeth Walton and Abigail Matthews. II. Title.
   PZ7.L56268Ad 2008
   [Fic]--dc22

                            2008014492

All Scripture quotations are taken from the Geneva Bible of 1599 or the King James Bible of 1611.

Editor: Barbara Scott
Art direction & cover design: Merit Alderink
Interior design: Carlos Eluterio Estrada
Cover Illustrator: Guy Porfirio

Printed in the United States of America

---

08 09 10 11 12 • 5 4 3 2 1

In Memory of My Mother,
Jane Meadows Oliver,
Who Always Halved Her Portion with Me

London, England

JUNE 12, 1609

Dearest Abigail,

If I were not at the harbor myself to tell you good-bye, I would not believe my dearest friend in the entire world is gone. I stayed and watched until your ship, the *Blessing*, and the other eight ships sailed out of sight.

You always were the first to try new things, but I never thought you would leave your homeland to travel to such an unknown land, and you are just twelve! I wish I could go with you.

My brother, John, could not take his eyes off the six horses and two mares that the captain ordered hoisted up in the air and over the edge of the pier onto the *Blessing*. Interesting company for your journey! One day you can tell your grandchildren you sailed the seas with Virginia's first horses.

However, for the life of me, I cannot understand how Temperance Flowerdew is going to make it in the New World. She is fearful of her very shadow. Now I know you do not like her much, but she is one of the few girls your age, and you will need her company. With that in mind, I gave her a grand farewell as she boarded her ship, the *Falcon*.

But why is it Temperance who will share your adventures and not I? I wish Papa had decided we could go too. Mother reminds me that she and Papa have plans for me that include a proper marriage to an educated and propertied gentleman of their choosing as soon as I am old enough. But I am only thirteen now — marriage is years away. In the meantime, I am to learn the "necessary accomplishments" — the ladylike arts of needlework and music — so that I may become a suitable prospect.

If only I could go to this New World with you. Perhaps we could make it into one where girls, not just boys, study things necessary to the building of the New World. Perhaps we could even go to

school like John does. I say we establish a new law for the colony (and for all those left in London who wish they were in the colony): *Henceforth and forevermore, young ladies may learn things necessary for the establishment of the well-being of the colony—government, law, architecture, mathematics, and science.*

Alas, soon Mr. Sewell, my disagreeable tutor, will arrive to instruct me in the *Book of Common Prayer*, and then Mother has more needlework for me to do. Brother John, however, tutored in many subjects I can only hope to read about one day, now goes to school most of the day. And then he shall have the finest education at Oxford University. I know Papa made sure I learned to read and write, and for that, I am truly grateful. If only Papa would let the tutor teach me what John studies. Why give me the key to this incredible world of learning but lock me away from everything it could open?

Dear friend, I already miss you so much! You were the only one who really understood this heart's desire and who did not mock me for it. Your heart for adventure is taking you far, far away from me and I cannot bear it. If only I was on that ship with you.

Your friend,

Elizabeth

Chipping Camden, England

JULY 12, 1609

Dear Abigail,

It has been exactly one month since you left, and I long for a letter from you. Papa has heard nothing either. Surely as one of the stockholders of the Virginia Company that sponsored your fleet, he would be among the first to learn of your arrival. I miss you so much. This waiting to learn of your safe passage is unbearable.

Papa sent me to the country to stay with my aunt and uncle. Ever since the fever that killed so many children in London four years ago, Papa whisks me out of the city and into the country air as much as possible during the summer. I do not mind though. Uncle has an exquisite library, and he has told me I may read anything here I desire. I only wish Papa felt the same way. They may be brothers, but their ideas of education are worlds apart.

I escape for long walks in the woods until I find just the right spot to spend an entire afternoon reading. I am fond of books about nature at present.

Write soon, dear friend! I miss you so.

Devotedly,

Elizabeth

Somewhere in the Atlantic Ocean

JULY 25, 1609

Dear Elizabeth,

This note must be short, and I do not know if you will ever have an opportunity to read it. But even if I drown, there is still a chance that this note could reach you. I want you to know that you have been my dearest friend ever, and I love you.

We are experiencing terrible gales and winds. The ship lists from side to side, and we are deathly afraid it will blow over. All hands are on deck—even Father—and he is not a sailor. I heard someone say it is a hurricane. If it is, we may all be doomed. Oh dearest Elizabeth, have I left my home and friends only to die on the way to my adventure? I must go. We are all needed to bail water.

Your friend forever,
even in heaven,

Abigail

Chipping Camden, England

JULY 28, 1609

Dear Abigail,

Still no word! I received a letter from Papa yesterday with great hopes that one from you would be tucked inside. But nothing! Papa said there is still no word about the fate of the ship on which you sailed. He does not say much, but I can tell he is worried too. I suppose it is too soon for letters to arrive from Virginia, but we were hoping for some word from a passing ship that arrived in London.

Today my aunt and I traveled by coach to the market. We spent a goodly part of the day overseeing the sale of our wool, spun into the softest yarn in the country. My job was to collect the coins and make the change. I was glad my aunt trusted me to do the proper figures and to keep the books for our sales. In the late afternoon, just before the close of the market, we purchased soap, cinnamon, writing paper, ink, wax candles, and some silk stockings for my aunt from a traveling merchant.

I know I prattle on about my comings and goings in my letters. It is a simple life here, but one where my education is valued. My aunt does not say it in so many words, but I do believe she thinks it is important to learn. Tonight I found a copy of a new book she left by my bedside: *A Booke of Divers Medecines* by Mrs. Corylon. Perhaps she saw my collection of medicinal herbs in the basket in the window. I could never be a physician or even an apothecary, as that is for men, but I do love to learn how to make remedies.

Your friend,

Elizabeth

On Solid Ground in the Colony of Virginia

AUGUST 18, 1609

Dearest Elizabeth,

I must write this posthaste even though it will be weeks, perhaps months before you receive this letter. Mother and Father and I are well—but many have been lost.

Several weeks into our journey, the sky darkened to a deep black. The wind tossed the *Blessing* to and fro for three days. Our ship lost contact with all the others. The blackness of the night continued even into day as waves as high as the sky washed over the deck.

As the hull filled with water, women and children below took buckets, scooped water from the body of the ship and handed them to the next person in line. At the end of the line below the deck, one of the men lifted them up to the other men on the deck, who threw the water overboard. Our courageous captain instructed all of us in what to do. He never appeared frightened. But I was terrified.

Finally, the winds calmed down. We had not slept for three days, and we were all surprised that the *Blessing* was still afloat. We cheered our captain who, though weary, was much relieved. The captain recharted our course. It seems that Admiral Somers had instructed the captains to head to Bermuda if the ships became separated.

A week after the winds calmed, the *Blessing* caught up with the *Lion* and the *Falcon*. I was ever so glad to see Temperance Flowerdew on the deck of the *Falcon*. The *Unity* was sore distressed—only the captain and one poor sailor were left alive. As the winds were strong for Virginia, the captains of the ships decided to head that way. We landed just one week ago. Yesterday, the *Diamond* and then the *Sparrow* docked. The *Sparrow* was barely afloat. The only ships left to arrive are the *Sea Venture* and one small supply vessel. There was great joy when we all were on the ground again, but our rejoicing was short-lived.

The wonderful new home we were all looking forward to is in great distress. Many of the people in the colony are sick. The colony is ill-prepared for so many new arrivals. There is precious little food or shelter. The bugs are horrible. I swat at my face and arms most of the day. It is hot and miserable.

Father speaks in hushed tones with Mother about the Indians as well. I know they are as fearful as I am. We heard that some of the Indians trade with the English, but there have been many more reports of the savagery of some of the tribes. No English girls have been here before. Will they leave us alone or kidnap us? Father says I must always stay inside the fort. He must be worried too.

Last night I heard the snap of a branch underfoot. I held my breath. Did I imagine it? Was it a deer? Or were they out there — at the palisade fence walls of the fort? Watching? Waiting? Please pray for us!

Your friend,

Abigail

Chipping Camden, England

AUGUST 22, 1609

Dear Abigail,

Tomorrow I leave for London. Uncle slipped me a present wrapped in paper and tied with a string. He says I am not to open it until I return to London. I have felt around the edges. It is a book! I wonder which one it is?

Oh, my dear, dear uncle. He probably knows it is the last book of any interest that I shall be allowed to read for a while. Soon Master Sewell will come calling to instruct me in the Christian faith and music, but nothing more. My mind simply must have more to fill it.

I am eager to learn everything I can about this world. Papa told me John will study astronomy this year in school. I too want to learn about the heavens and the stars. Why is it only something a boy can learn? I am good at figures. I could calculate the paths of stars. If only Papa would let me.

Tonight, however, I did not study the stars—I danced under them. Our coach arrived at Heathcoate Manor at six o'clock. I wore a violet damask gown trimmed with lace. You remember it? It is the one Mother bought for me at the Royal Exchange this spring. My aunt lent me a necklace of amethysts and pearls that glistened in the moonlight against my dress. She helped comb my hair and my ordinarily unruly curls looked beautiful as they spilled down on my neck.

Apparently, some of the young gentlemen thought I looked agreeable as well for I danced nearly every dance! I wish you had been there. It would have made it all so much more wonderful to have shared this evening with you.

Tomorrow I journey home to London—and hopefully, to news about you.

Your friend,

Elizabeth

James Towne, Virginia

August 26, 1609

Dear Elizabeth,

We are hungry. The food we had on the ships spoiled from the seawater getting into it. We have no place to sleep but under the stars. Many are sick. The new leaders of the colony, with orders from the king to govern the colony, are on the *Sea Venture*, and it has not yet arrived. There is much bickering among the leaders about who will govern if the *Sea Venture* has been lost. No wonder the king wanted to replace these leaders with new ones.

With each week that passes, we grow more anxious about the *Sea Venture*. I overheard Mother trying to comfort Mistress Pierce. She fears her husband, who traveled with the other leaders on it, is lost. What would it be like for little Jane to lose her father so young? I could not imagine life without Father, not in this fearful place.

Captain John Smith is furious with other so-called leaders, especially Captain Ratcliffe. He took men to Point Comfort to build a stockade. Others have been sent out to look for food.

I must close now. I hope you have heard word of the *Sea Venture* and that they are safe as well. Little Jane cries herself to sleep each night with worry about her father.

Your friend,

Abigail

London, England

Dearest Abigail,

I have been worried sick. Oh, how I hate to wait for news. I pray you made it there safely and that I will hear from you before too long. Mother tells me I should think good thoughts of you and not the worst, and so I will.

I imagine the colonists there were quite happy to see all the ships arrive. What did they think of the horses? Where are you living? Did you find a wonderful home waiting for you? Please give my love to your dear parents, and know that I am thinking of you now in August, no matter when you actually receive this letter.

Master Sewell arrives tomorrow, and my dreaded tutoring begins again. Mother greeted me upon my return from Uncle's home, asked all about my time in Chipping Camden, and then promptly put some new needlework in my hands. I wish it were a book she put in my hands instead.

That reminded me of Uncle's present. Tonight after I bade my parents good night, I opened his present. Yes, it was a book, but I was quite surprised at what he had sent to me. It is a New Testament — in Greek! I knew instantly why he had chosen it.

Tomorrow I shall approach Papa with utmost decorum and in my most persuasive manner seek his leave to study the Greek language with Master Sewell. Oh, how can Papa object to such a singular request of one eager to learn more of her faith in its original language? Uncle is so dear and so clever!

Your devoted friend,

Elizabeth

James Towne, Virginia

AUGUST 31, 1609

Dear Elizabeth,

We are under much pressure now. Our two blacksmiths work night and day making nails for the new homes. The newcomers must build as many homes as possible inside the fort before winter. We will likely have several families in each home.

I hope we are with Captain and Mistress Pierce and little Jane. I am quite fond of them. Captain Tucker told Mistress Pierce that if anyone can survive a hurricane, it is Captain Pierce. Yet, we still have had no word about the *Sea Venture.*

For now, we are in a lean-to made of small trees and mats woven of reeds from the marsh. My fingers are cut all over from the effort. Mother and I soak the reeds in water until they are soft and then weave them back and forth until we have a strong, tight mat.

Father says our work will keep the rain from soaking us, and he keeps us in good spirits as we weave. Temperance is not at all interested in weaving mats. I do not think she was ready for this adventure at all.

Your friend,

Abigail

James Towne, Virginia

SEPTEMBER 2, 1609

Dear Elizabeth,

I just heard that a supply ship will return to England next week. I want to write as much as possible so my bundle of letters can reach you soon. I will write to you after our day's chores are finished. There is so much work to be done.

We have all but given up hope that the *Sea Venture* will be saved. It has been six weeks now, and no one has heard any word of the grand ship. All are feared dead. Mistress Pierce is very brave around Jane. At night, when Jane is asleep, I hear Mistress Pierce crying. Mother cares for her and comforts her. Poor Jane. I cannot imagine what it would be like without Father.

It seems most of the leaders are more interested in finding gold than finding food for the colonists. Father and Mother speak quietly about food. I know they are concerned. Mother squirrels away as much of her ration of dried fish cakes as she can preserve, but food spoils so easily in this heat.

Mother and Mistress Pierce try to garden, but as Mistress Pierce told Mother, the radish, onion, cucumber, and cabbage seeds salvaged from the journey are poor quality and have been sown late. We are not very hopeful.

I am trying to be nice to Temperance. I know you think she will be a friend and companion here, but there is not an ounce of adventure in her soul. She whimpers and frets and is simply not pleasant to be around. I will try, for your sake, to be her friend, but oh, she is tiresome. She worked beside me in a small garden plot today. All she could talk about was the market in London where she used to select her fresh apricots, cherries, and lettuces. Well, this certainly is *not* London. If we are to have vegetables at all, we must work to get them.

Your friend,

Abigail

James Towne, Virginia

SEPTEMBER 4, 1609

Dear Elizabeth,

Horrible things are happening here. Captain Martin of the *Falcon* and his men went upriver to trade with the Indians. He sent messengers to offer copper and hatchets for food, but the Indians killed them all! Captain Martin and his men took vengeance on the Indians, and a deadly battle began. Some say our settlement is in danger now, for the Indians will not let this attack by Captain Martin go unanswered.

Remember when we heard in London that the Indians were friendly? That they traded food with the men in the settlement willingly? Well, it simply is not true! Were we tricked into coming here—coming here to die?

Father looks very worried and keeps patting me on the shoulder as if he is trying to reassure himself that he made the right decision to bring us here. Mother talks with him in whispers. Are we going to die here? Will they shoot us full of arrows? Are the palisade walls strong enough to keep them out?

Do you remember meeting Henry Spelman on the London dock? He came over on the ships with us and is our age. Because he had no parents and came here to work, Captain John Smith took Henry with him on an expedition up the James River to the falls. Captain Smith bargained for a Powhatan village that is filled with dry houses for lodging and land ready to plant. As part of the bargain, Captain Smith gave them Henry! Apparently, this is a way to show good will. It is all too strange for me. But think how strange it must be for poor Henry!

On his way back, Captain Smith was horribly burned from an explosion. A spark ignited his gunpowder in a pouch at his waist. It is rumored he will return with the ships to England. Then who will govern? And what about poor Henry if Captain Smith is not there to retrieve him? Will the Indians treat him kindly without Captain Smith there to ensure his safety? What about us? With Captain Smith leaving for London, will the Indians think we are without protection as they watch our president sail away? Will that be a signal for them to gather in force to attack us? I am terribly afraid.

The only good thing about all this is that the ship that takes Captain Smith back to England will also carry my letters to you. I miss you dearly, Elizabeth. Tell your father that the state of things here in Virginia is not good at all. Beg him to do all in his power to convince the Company to send us supplies. The colony was not prepared for us, and now we number nearly 500 souls. This new world is not at all what was described to us in London.

Your friend,

Abigail

James Towne, Virginia

OCTOBER 28, 1609

Dear Elizabeth,

I have nothing but bad news to give you. So many dreadful
things are happening so fast. We learned that the winters can
be very cold here. Last winter the bitter winds layered the deep
snow with ice. Because the fort is so close to the water, the winter
gales pierce the palisade walls and torture those inside with icy
sharpness.

James Towne has other problems. As soon as Captain Smith was
injured, George Percy took over as president. President Percy sent
Mr. Ratcliffe and fifty soldiers to negotiate with Chief Powhatan
for corn. At first it seemed the negotiations were going well. Chief
Powhatan traded bread and venison for copper and blue glass beads.
He even offered lodging for the men.

The next day, our men collected grain at the Indian storehouses.
When Mr. Ratcliffe noticed that the Indians were using their
hands to push up the bottom of the woven baskets to measure the
grain and cheat us of the full measure, he was outraged. Words
were exchanged, and tempers flared. Then Chief Powhatan came
out of a lodge with Henry Spelman! Henry must have been so
very frightened. He had been traded once from the English to the
Powhatans. What would happen now? Was he to be killed because
of these angry Englishmen?

Mr. Ratcliffe ended the trading, and with the corn they already
had, headed for their ship, the *Discovery*. Then they were ambushed!
The Indians killed them one by one. They tried to capture the ship
as well. Only sixteen of the traders returned to the ship, and Henry
Spelman was not with them.

I spoke with Father about all of this. I am terrified of the
Indians. Though he was reluctant to tell me, Father explained that
the English were not free of fault. They had killed many Indian

women and children out of vengeance and spite. I was horrified to learn this. Father would not tell me more, but said that often things are not what they seem.

I will think about this.

Your friend,

Abigail

James Towne, Virginia

November 16, 1609

Dear Elizabeth,

More troubles. Captain Francis West and his crew of forty men sailed upriver in the *Swallow* to trade with the Indians near the Potomac. They were friendly Indians, but Captain West killed many of them and burned their villages. Then on the way back, with their ship loaded with corn for James Towne, they stopped at Point Comfort. There they stole the *Swallow* and sailed for England. Cowards all!

This rebellion is a terrible blow to the colony. We need the ship and the corn. We certainly need good relations with friendly Indians. What Captain West did will only convince the Indians that we are their dangerous enemies. That is not all. They sailed without giving me a chance to send you my last letters.

President Percy ordered Master Potts to take an inventory of how much food there is for the colony. It does not look good. I heard Father tell Mother there is only half a can of corn meal a day for each person in the colony for three months. That is not nearly enough to get us through the winter.

Mother continues to work with Mistress Pierce digging for roots and berries that can be dried for the winter. She tries to stay in good spirits, but I can tell she is worried.

I do have a bit of good news. We are sharing a home with Mistress Pierce and Jane. Captain Tucker made sure of it. He and Father are good friends now after having built so many homes together these last few months. Father says that although he knew Captain Tucker in London, it is here under the Virginia sun that their friendship has been sealed.

Mother enjoys the companionship of Mistress Pierce, who knows more about gardening than anyone else here. Mistress Pierce often clucks her tongue, wishing that she had been here in the spring during planting season. She brought with her a number of boxes of seeds from her garden in England. She hopes the seawater that washed into the *Blessing* did not destroy the life in those seeds. If they are all right, she tells Mother, then by this time next year, we will have cabbages, turnips, onions, and carrots. Right now all we have is a bit of meal made from these horrible root vegetables. Mother tells me this is what the Indians eat.

Your friend,

Abigail

London, England

Dearest Abigail,

Papa just brought me your letters! The captain of the *Blessing* gave them to him at a meeting for the Virginia Company members. The very ship that took you away now has returned to London with Captain Smith and such dire news.

I stayed up very late hoping my candles would last so I could read each one of your letters. My dear, dear friend, I am so afraid for you.

I cannot believe that the colony is so distressed. And the *Sea Venture*! Such a terrible loss for us all. Now Captain Smith has been injured. What will the colony do? We had such high hopes this summer. Now all the leaders that were chosen to govern the colony are lost at sea! This is tragic, tragic news.

At least you and your family are safe. Mother thanks God over and over for that good news in the midst of such pain and grief. She and Papa lost some very dear friends on the *Sea Venture*. Papa says the Company will send Lord De La Warr to the colony as quickly as possible with supplies and additional men. Everyone here is heartbroken over the loss of such honorable men, women, and children.

John does not yet understand all the implications of this tragedy. He was excited to find out that the Captain of the *Blessing* has returned to London as he wants to know about the horses and how they fare now.

You remain constantly in my prayers, and I remain,

Your devoted friend,

Elizabeth

London, England

December 10, 1609

Dear Abigail,

For the last week I have read your letters over and over again. Your life there in Virginia is so much different than we both expected. I thought you would arrive, settle quickly into a new home much like yours here, and pick up with your life with nothing changed—except the place. How silly and ignorant of me.

I let Mother read your letters, and she lingered over them. I think she is trying to put herself in your mother's place and understand all that your family endures there. Papa mentioned tonight that the gold sent back to London from Virginia was nothing but fool's gold. The Company, which had great hopes for finding valuable ore there in Virginia, was sorely disappointed.

I think we all wonder if this is a fool's errand in trying to establish an English colony in such a dangerous place. Mother murmured that perhaps it was too soon to send wives and children to the colony. Papa just puffed harder on his pipe, but I could tell he agreed. I know they fear for the safety of your family.

I shall continue to write to you of my life, but I fear it seems insensitive of me to tell you of my troubles, which are nothing compared to your own. Papa would not let me study Greek—not even the Greek New Testament. He says that I will not have any need for it, so it would be a waste of my time. I know I shall never be able to attend Oxford or Cambridge to study, but I have such a hunger to learn.

I mentioned to him that Queen Elizabeth had been well versed in languages both modern and ancient, and had studied Greek as well as Latin. Papa only puffed harder on his pipe and turned away. After a few moments he said, "Elizabeth, you were named for that honorable sovereign, but that does not mean you are destined for her calling. She studied what she needed for her calling to rule

26

England. You must study what you need for your calling to rule your household and maids one day."

I was furious at him. Cannot he see that I am destined for greatness too? Is it the misfortune of my birth which offends? If only I was born a boy. My brother, John, by virtue of the chance of his birth, shall have all the advantages—the best tutors, the best schools—and I shall have none.

Papa must have talked to Mother about it because for weeks afterwards I had additional lessons on the lute and recorder, extra sessions with Master Sewell in Christian instruction, and a pile of needlework. I suppose their plan is to keep me so busy that I will forget all about these other notions. I wish I was back at Uncle's home where at least I could read what I wanted.

I fear I must sound so selfish. I am crossing my arms and stamping my foot about not getting to learn something new, and you are trying to survive in a cold and distant land. Forgive me, my dear friend.

Your friend,
Elizabeth

London, England

DECEMBER 17, 1609

Dear Abigail,

As part of mother's plan to keep my education focused on learning how to run and manage a household, she has taken me with her to the Royal Exchange today to shop. I did not mind, though, because the shopping today was for your family!

I admired Mother's wisdom as she selected plain but sturdy fabrics, strong leather shoes and boots for each of you, and comfortable shirts and smocks. I watched her pass over the lace and silk garments to select linen, wool, and hempen fabrics. She says they will be more practical for the life you now lead. I watched her fingers linger over kidskin gloves, and I could tell she was thinking of your mother. She selected warm wool gloves and mittens instead.

Mother quickly worked her way through the vendors and selected hazelnuts and chestnuts, salt, cinnamon, soap, needles, thread, candles, and paper and ink (for us!).

My job was to record the purchases, calculate the prices, and count the change. These activities, Mother says, will be necessary when I wed and manage my household. Well, at least I could use arithmetic. I must confess, though, I admired my mother greatly today. Her decisions were swift and wise. Her selections were perfectly suited for your family's new life. I admit I have much to learn from her.

Papa will make sure these arrive on the next ship to Virginia. It is soon to be Christmas. I miss you especially now.

Your friend,

Elizabeth

James Towne, Virginia

CHRISTMAS DAY, 1609

Dear Elizabeth,

I can almost smell the goose cooking and taste the rich plum pudding. You are most certainly eating wondrous foods in the warmth of your home. We had a paste of meal and water that Mother baked and then tried to make festive with a myrtle leaf perkily sticking out of the bread.

Father continues to try to keep up our spirits. He read from his Bible of the wondrous birth of our Lord, and he reminded us that God still does miracles today. We need a miracle, Elizabeth, or we will all die. Four more dear souls died this very day. One was but a young child. This does not seem at all like Christmas.

For Mother, I will try to remain happy, but I am very worried about her. She seems so very frail.

Your friend,

Abigail

London, England

Dear Abigail,

These last few weeks have been filled with parties. I missed you especially one night when we played your favorite card game, Laugh and Lie Down, for hours on end. Papa gave us a new deck of cards he had just bought. The cards had illustrations on the backs of each card of the Gunpowder Rebellion of a few years ago. When he passed them to me, he mentioned that I might be interested in reading the backs of the cards. I wonder what this means? He has never mentioned my learning any history before.

Mother and I took food and blankets when we visited the poor this week. It made me wish that our supplies were already in your hands, but alas, no ship has yet sailed for Virginia.

Mother supervised the decorating of the house with holly boughs, ivy vines, and sprigs of mistletoe. We decorated our wassail bowl with rosemary sprigs and ribbon. More household education of Elizabeth! It is also my job to keep the Yule log burning.

Sometimes I think Papa will soften and let me learn a few things other than becoming an acceptable prospect for wife and mother. I am fourteen now, and in my mind, years away from marriage, but Papa thinks these next few years will go quickly.

At our party, Papa stood by proudly as I played the virginals for our guests and accompanied the carol singers. I have to admit that years of lessons have done their work. My fingers sailed over the keys and the wondrous sounds from the plucked strings filled the room. Papa beamed with pride. I am doomed.

Your dutiful friend,

Elizabeth

James Towne, Virginia

JANUARY 13, 1610

Dear Elizabeth,

You would have been proud of me today. I visited Temperance. She is so ill. She did not prattle on as she usually does. I brought her a linen handkerchief that survived the hurricane. I had worked her initials in thread pulled from the hem of Mother's brightest dress. Temperance lifted her hand in a gesture of thanks, but she was too weak to say much more.

Her eyes were very red, and I could see that she had been crying for a long time. I surprised myself by taking her in my arms to let her sob. I know how she feels.

This is a very scary time. Many people die each day. There is no more food. We are eating rats, snakes, acorns, and roots. There are those who have run out from the fort in desperation looking for food, only to be killed by the Indians. We are prisoners inside this fort—prisoners of our own hunger.

The old-timers tell of a young Indian princess called Pocahontas who used to visit and was kind to them. But no one has seen her for a long time. I wish she would help us get food.

Hunger does strange things to people. At first your stomach twists and turns in such pain. Then it becomes quiet—almost too quiet. Today a man ate his shoes. Another man ate his dog.

We began as 500 souls, but we are becoming fewer and fewer. The dead are buried at night so the Indians will not know how few of us are left. Many are near death. Mother is confined to bed now. She is too weak to get up. I make her a soup of some sticks, a few acorns, and some leaves. It is not soup at all! It is a vain attempt to convince us all we are not going to die! But that is not going to happen, is it? It is just a matter of time before we are all dead. Must we watch as the ones we love suffer so greatly? Is there no hope?

I have to hold Mother's head up so she can sip the soup. She smiles at me weakly. Father does not say much. He and Captain Tucker speak in hushed tones.

I am very frightened. I know I should depend on God now more than ever, but if anything were to happen to my dear parents, I do not know what I would do.

We have heard word that Lord De La Warr will be coming soon. Supplies are desperately needed here. I trust that by the time you can read through the entire bundle of letters, there will be a happy ending. I miss reading with you, Elizabeth. It seems so long ago that we read stories of life-threatening adventures and maidens rescued by heroes. Now I am living that adventure. I just need a hero.

Your very frightened friend,

Abigail

James Towne, Virginia

JANUARY 19, 1610

Dear Elizabeth,

Mother is much weaker. She can no longer sit up even for my pretend soup. Her skin is clammy, and her face is flushed. Mistress Pierce wrings out cloths of cool water to put on her fevered brow. I stand by so helpless.

I decided I had to do something to help Mother. I will not be able to bear it if she does not get better. So, long after nightfall, I found a hole in the palisade wall of the fort. It was a hole just the right size for me to slip through.

When I had one foot and one shoulder through the wall, a strong hand clamped down on my other shoulder. It was Captain Tucker on night guard duty. He has the awful duty of rationing out the remaining food supplies. He must do so even though mothers with starving children cling to him begging for more than their day's share.

I turned and looked into his eyes. They were as warm as his hand was forceful.

"Where do you think you are going, young lady?" he said sternly.

"I must find Mother some food. I can bear it no longer. If she does not get some food soon, she will die."

Captain Tucker pulled me back through the wall. "Abigail, your father is a good man. What do you think it would do to him if he lost you as well as his wife? Come, I have something to show you."

I walked with him to the other side of the fort where he knocked the snow off a tarp covering a large lump. It was the beginnings of a small ship!

"I have been working on this at night in secret."

"Captain Tucker! This is a large boat. Could it be big enough for—"

"Trading?" answered Captain Tucker. "I think so. Now, you

must not tell a soul as I do not want anyone taking off in this boat before I have a chance to go upriver to trade for corn with the friendlier Indians. I still have some more work to do on it. Can you keep my secret?"

I nodded. Then Captain Tucker reached in his pocket and gave me seven kernels of corn. "For your mother, Abigail. And for you — to hope again."

I ran home with tears in my eyes. I am so happy. Soon we may have plenty of corn!

Your hopeful friend,

Abigail

James Towne, Virginia

FEBRUARY 16, 1610

Dear Elizabeth,

Remember when I told you about my gift of corn three weeks ago? When I went home, Mother slowly chewed each kernel of Captain Tucker's corn. She wanted it to last and last. The next day, she was able to sit up again to take some of my pretend soup. She even laughed with me and said, "Let's pretend this is goose soup. Mmmm. So hot and delicious." It was so good to hear her laugh.

But now, Father paces the floor and checks on Mother every few minutes. She has taken a turn for the worse. It is so cold, and Mother is skin and bones now. She cannot stay warm. There is not much we can do. Many people die each day. Others are weak from starvation and illness. I have been praying so hard for Mother. Why is she getting worse? Does God not hear my prayers?

Father reads his Bible for long stretches of time. He seems greatly troubled. I have heard him talk very quietly with Captain Tucker outside the house. He said, "There must be a way" and "I have to do something."

But what, Elizabeth, can he possibly do?

Your friend,

Abigail

James Towne, Virginia

February 17, 1610

Dear Elizabeth,

I am so frightened. Father and Captain Tucker left during the night, and they have not returned. Mistress Pierce just hugs me all day as we sit together and watch poor Mother. Mistress Pierce told me that my father felt so helpless, watching his blessed wife waste away day after day, unable to do anything about it.

I know exactly how Father is feeling. I know with his lion's heart, he would do anything to protect Mother and me. I hope Father is just going to forage in the woods and not to try to trade with the Indians. Word has it that Chief Powhatan has instructed all his tribes not to trade with the English and to kill them if they have the opportunity.

Oh, Elizabeth, I am trying to trust God in this.

Your friend,

Abigail

London, England
FEBRUARY 22, 1610

Dear Abigail,

I have not heard from you in such a long time. No ships have gone or come from Virginia. Lord De La Warr was supposed to take the next supply to the colony, but he has been ill, so the trip was delayed. Mother has arranged and rearranged the packages she prepared for your family two months ago. She is anxious to get these supplies to you.

Today the entire Virginia Company gathered at Temple Church to commission Lord De La Warr as governor of the colony and to pray for the new colonists soon to set sail for Virginia. Papa was there and said Reverend Crashaw preached a mighty sermon.

He said we have a duty to support those in Virginia in four things: countenance, person, purse, and prayer. He reminded everyone that we must not become discouraged from reports from the colony as God can make something of small beginnings. He urged the Company to send honorable persons to the colony to assist its growth and that the Company should not expect to profit yet from the colony, but rather serve the colony with needful supplies. I, for one, will do my duty to God to pray for Lord De La Warr, as I know he is going to help my dearest friend.

When you last listened to Reverend Crashaw, your family decided to become adventurers too. As I watched you then, I wondered what was going on in your heart. Your eyes were glistening with tears. Were you afraid? Were you anxious? Were you feeling the tug in your heart that the Lord wanted you to trust him in this new adventure too?

Do not stop trusting him now.

Your friend,

Elizabeth

James Towne, Virginia

Dear Elizabeth,

Captain Tucker returned last night with Father on his shoulders. He was pierced by Indian arrows and had lost a great deal of blood. Captain Tucker carried him to his lodge, because we did not want Mother to know. Captain Tucker and Mistress Pierce attended to Father's wounds.

When Father called out for me, Mistress Pierce brought me close to him. He grabbed my hand and said, "Do not lose faith. God will look after you whatever happens. Trust him with all your heart, and he will not forsake you." Then he died!

I could not believe it! I had braced myself to lose my precious mother, but my father as well? I felt weak and terrified. My whole world has turned upside down. My father, gone? I cannot bear it!

Temperance came when we buried Father. She hugged me and said I should come to her home where I could cry for Father. My tears would be too much for Mother. I moved numbly through the burial, but when she said that, the floodgates opened. I sobbed and sobbed till there was nothing left but wrenching agony.

Temperance held me until my tears were spent. I was never so grateful for a friend. She is right. I must not show any sadness to Mother now. If she knew about Father, the grief would surely kill her.

It was Father who always kept our family strong. He was the one who encouraged us when we were afraid. Oh, Elizabeth, what if Mother dies too? What will I do if I have neither father nor mother! I cannot bear the thought.

In deep agony,

Abigail

James Towne, Virginia

MARCH 1, 1610

Dear Elizabeth,

Mother is still ill, and she still does not know about Father. Captain Tucker and Mistress Pierce explained to me that the shock would be too much for her. We must give her every reason to live.

Mistress Pierce suggested I sit with her and talk with her as if nothing were wrong. It is so strange to do this, but I will do it for Father. He would want me to do everything possible to help Mother live.

Mother only wakens from her stupor a few moments each day. She touches my face or hand. "Your father?" she asks.

I gather all my strength to respond, "Captain Tucker is with him." It is not a lie, is it? Captain Tucker did lay him down in the ground, and covered him over with dirt.

I do not know if I can do this. The pain is unbearable. But I must not lose Mother too. I cannot. God cannot let that happen. Not now.

With deep sadness,

Abigail

London, England

MARCH 1, 1610

Dear Abigail,

Finally. Today Lord De La Warr and nearly 150 men with additional supplies left London. I cannot forget what you said about how little food there is in the colony. How ill-prepared the colony was to receive you all! Captain Smith's reports to the Virginia Company stockholders only confirmed how desperate the situation is.

Oh, dear Abigail, I am so hopeful now that I know Lord De La Warr has set sail. I will pray faithfully each day that he reaches your family in time. Soon you will have my letters and our packages — and food.

The "education of Elizabeth for wifely enterprises" continues in force. It seems that perhaps my interest in herbs and plants this summer will not go to waste as Mother has determined to teach me how to make remedies. She wants me to accompany her on her charitable journeys to visit the poor. We will administer our remedies to those who are ill.

Today, Mother taught me how to make a potion from comfrey root and licorice to clear up the lungs.

Your friend,

Elizabeth

James Towne, Virginia

MARCH 3, 1610

Dear Elizabeth,

Last night, we were all asleep when I heard Mother stirring. I leapt up from the floor and came quickly to her side. She moved slightly and motioned for me to lie down beside her. I held her and sang to her the song she had sung to me all these years:

> *My little one, my precious one, do you know God loves you?*
> *My little one, my precious one, do you know he cares?*
> *He always is with you— in the dawn and in the night.*
> *He will never leave you, nor forsake you,*
> *He will guide you to his light.*

I stroked her hair and thought of all she has done for me in my life. There was no greater sacrifice than the one she made for me during this horrible, horrible winter. Before we ran out of food, Mother shared her daily ration with me. I saw her cut back on her portion to give me more. I protested strongly, but Mother would hear nothing of it. Each day, she gave up some of her food so I could live. But what is my life without hers?

I continued to stroke her hair and sing to her. Then as the morning sun was rising, she slipped away to heaven. Mistress Pierce had been up all night as well, but said nothing to me. She knew this time with Mother—these last few moments—was to be all mine.

We buried Mother today. I returned, an orphan, to our home in James Towne. When I could cry no longer, I turned my face to the wall. I tried to shut out the thoughts that tormented my mind and the terrifying fear that gripped my heart. What will happen to me now?

Your friend,

Abigail

London, England

APRIL 19, 1610

Dear Abigail,

We learned Lord De La Warr took a shorter course. He should be in Virginia sooner than expected. I will feel so much better once I know you are well. The *Godspeed* leaves from London next month, and I will send another bundle of letters with it when it sails.

Mother has prepared another package for your mother. She collected seeds for turnips, cabbages, radishes, cucumbers, apples, pears, and cherries. She is determined that your mother's garden shall be the best in the colony. I noticed a hoe, several trowels, and brand-new garden gloves tucked in a corner of the kitchen. I suspect she will find a way to get those to your family as well.

I will add more paper and ink and some fresh quills. I wish I knew what else would be helpful to you. I long for more letters from you. Supply ships are sailing more frequently between the colony and here. Perhaps now our letters will speed their way to each other with great haste.

Your hopeful friend,

Elizabeth

James Towne, Virginia

MAY 4, 1610

Dear Elizabeth,

I could not write to you for awhile after Mother died. The grief has been too much to bear. Whenever I tried, my tears spilled onto the paper and smeared the ink. I crumpled up the letters and threw them against the wall. I was so angry, and yet I could not compose myself enough to share with you, my dearest friend, what I have been feeling.

I will try again now, for I long for your company again. I know you must have been frightened for us when you heard the news about Captain Smith and the sad state of the colony. Yet we have had no word from England or any hope of assistance since September—eight months ago!

My heart is burdened with grief. I spend many days crying. Mistress Pierce holds me until my eyes are too tired to cry any more. She told me I will continue to live at their house. Captain Tucker spoke with President Percy who agreed to this, at least until passage to England can be arranged. Mistress Pierce has been very kind to me, but I have made up my mind. I am an English girl, and I will return to England. I will forget this place ever existed—if it can continue to exist at all.

I do not know what I will do as an orphan or where I will live. I just want to be on English soil again and to see you. Perhaps Uncle Samuel will take me in at Warwickshire.

The settlement is greatly troubled, Elizabeth. There are no supplies, no food, and no relief from London. The rats scavenged what few provisions we had left. We are imprisoned inside the fort. We cannot fish. We cannot hunt. We cannot grow food. Oh, for a handful of corn!

Those hateful Powhatans will not trade with us. They simply wait for anyone who dares to come outside the fort. Then they kill

them—just as they did Father. One day the Powhatans promised to trade for corn. Several of our men agreed to leave the safety of the fort to make the trade. They were all killed. Those Powhatans are wicked tricksters!

It is horrible inside the fort. Men eat dogs, rats, snakes, anything they can to stay alive. Do not tell poor John, but there is not a horse left alive now.

Before the winter, we numbered 500, but with the warmth of spring, only about sixty of us are left. I am so thin and very heartsick after losing Father and Mother, but I refuse to die. I will see you again. I hunger to return to London. Soon, very soon, I will be able to come home.

Temperance is also going home. Just as soon as the next ship arrives, if we can make it that long. We will come home together. I promise I will never, ever say another bad thing about Temperance.

One needs more than a spirit of adventure to survive in this dreaded place. I miss you so much, Elizabeth, but soon, I will be with you again. That thought alone will keep me alive. I will think of England and the River Thames and reading poetry with you.

Your very English friend,
who is no more an adventurer,

Abigail

James Towne, Virginia

MAY 16, 1610

Dear Elizabeth,

Mistress Pierce is so thin. She has been as true to me as Mother. She continues to halve her portion of nuts or dried berries with Jane and me. She is very careful to protect from decay the stores of dried nuts and berries that she and Mother had gathered. Although we nibble on just a small ration each day, it sustains us. Few, though, are left alive.

Captain Tucker, our cape merchant, stopped by twice in recent weeks to bring us a special ration of a dried fish cake. His shallop boat is now finished, and he is ready to take it out to trade.

President Percy, however, has decided that he will take the shallop and go to Point Comfort to see how those there fared during this awful time. All are more hopeful now. Captain Tucker's shallop is large enough for us to escape if aid does not come soon.

Your soon-to-be-across-the-Atlantic friend,

Abigail

James Towne, Virginia

MAY 18, 1610

Dear Elizabeth,

I am so furious I could scream. President Percy and Captain Tucker returned from Fort Algernon at Point Comfort. A few soldiers were sent there months ago. I had feared for their lives and had wondered if President Percy would find anyone alive.

I wasted my concern. Captain Tucker reported that almost all were fit as a fiddle and enjoying the abundance of crabs and oysters found along the shore! President Percy was furious too. I overheard him tell Captain Tucker that the crabs these men fed to their hogs would have been a great relief to us and saved many lives.

Those men also kept two of the small ships, the *Virginia* and the *Discovery*, for fishing in the bay. Just think what Captain Tucker could have done with those ships if they had been at James Towne! Selfish, selfish men.

President Percy decided he would take half of us, about thirty, to the Point for food. When that group recovers, the other half will go to the Point. We are all so near death, we will risk venturing outside the fort for the promise of food. If all else fails, we will abandon this dreadful colony. President Percy speaks well when he says that another town or fort can be built, but men's lives, once lost, can never be recovered.

Captain Tucker wants Mistress Pierce, Jane, and me to go in the first half, but we protested. There are others in much worse straits than we are. We can wait another few weeks.

If the truth be known, I do not know what I would do to those men if I saw them—fat and happy, while almost all in the colony starved to death. They were so selfish and unwilling to share the food or the ships. If Father could have had that ship for one day, I know he could have found fish for Mother. I am so angry. These are

people with no souls who only think of themselves and fatten their bellies while those nearby starved.

With men like that, this colony cannot survive.

Your furious friend,

Abigail

James Towne, Virginia

MAY 23, 1610

Dear Elizabeth,

I will stay up all night and use three candles if I have to in order to write you this amazing news. The *Sea Venture* landed today! Well, not really the *Sea Venture* itself. It was shipwrecked in Bermuda. But all were not lost!

Early in the morning, a sentry on the fort spotted two small ships drifting to James Towne on calm waters. Captain Tucker told Mistress Pierce, Jane, and me to stay inside the house until it was known whether they were friend or foe.

Imagine our surprise when the new governor, Sir Thomas Gates, Admiral Somers, Vice Admiral Newport, and all the others from the *Sea Venture* walked down the planks from the ships. All save two who boarded the *Sea Venture* in London a year ago are safe!

They arrived in two small ships called the *Patience* and the *Deliverance*. Perfect names for these ships, I think. We ran out to meet them, but they looked at us in horror. I think we looked like skeletons in ragged clothing. That was when I noticed. Every one of the *Sea Venture* passengers looked healthy and well fed.

Captain Tucker helped the women and children down from the ship, and we all gathered around to greet them. Then the men walked down the plank. Mistress Pierce gasped. There was Captain Pierce, as hale and hearty as ever. He swept little Jane up in his arms, and Mistress Pierce kept patting his arm as if she could not believe he was really standing there next to her.

The last man to leave the ship was Admiral Somers. He saw me standing alone and walked over to me. Admiral Somers asked after Father. When I shook my head and looked away, he put his strong hand on my shoulder. After a moment, I turned back to him and

48

said simply, "Mother too." He sighed deeply, gave one sweeping glance around the fort, and sighed again.

I know your parents will want to know about the Rolfes. Mistress Rolfe survived the awful voyage and gave birth to a daughter soon after landing on Bermuda. Reverend Bucke, their dear friend, christened their baby girl Bermuda. She died several days later. The Rolfes are heartbroken.

The church bell rang out, and everyone gathered for prayer. Reverend Bucke prayed for us all and wept openly at the devastation of our colony. He asked God to grant wisdom to our new governor, Sir Thomas Gates, and show us the way. I silently prayed the way would be straight back to England.

After the service, Master William Strachey read the governor's commission. President Percy surrendered his commission to Governor Gates. Now we will see what he decides will become of us.

Governor Gates walked around James Towne. He appeared shocked. Much of the palisade wall is in disrepair. The gates to the musket holes hang by a hinge. Of course, we had used the abandoned houses of those who died for firewood. I am sure President Percy filled him in on the situation with the terrible Indians as well.

Captain Pierce, Mistress Pierce, and little Jane walked arm in arm toward our home. I decided to stay with Temperance and give them some time together. Although I was very glad to see their family reunited, it made me miss Mother and Father all the more. I will not think about that today, however. Today is a day of great tales of adventure and miracles.

We gathered the *Sea Venture* colonists together to hear their tale. No one cared at that moment that there was still too little food for us plus the additional 150 new colonists. We were hungry for tales of bravery and survival.

Remember the hurricane that clipped all of the ships in the *Sea Venture*'s convoy? Well, the *Sea Venture* had the worst of it. Master William Strachey, long involved with the London theater, told the

tale. We all sat down on mats, and he leapt on a bench to tell the tale in a most dramatic fashion.

This is the story he told:

> The clouds gathered thick upon the *Sea Venture* and the winds were singing and whistling most unusually. A darkness came upon us that beat the light from heaven, and it turned terribly black. Every captain on board said we were in trouble. Admiral Somers, an experienced seaman, knew we were in the midst of a hurricane. From noon on Tuesday until Friday, the ship lurched from side to side as the winds blew us toward the dreaded Bermuda Islands. Many a ship has wrecked upon the reefs near those islands, never to be heard from again. Admiral Somers was at the helm, never sleeping, never standing down.

> It did not just rain. Oh, no. It was as if a river was flooding the air. Not only was the ship taking on water from the skies but the winds pushed the seawater in billowing waves over the ship's deck and into her hull. The women and children stayed below deck even as the water was rising rapidly. There was a mighty leak that caused the ship to draw five feet of water. The crew worked nonstop with pumps and buckets to try to clear the water from the ship's hold. Biscuits and meat were floating everywhere.

> Admiral Somers divided the men into three groups and told each man where to stand. Every man took the bucket or pump for one hour and then rested for the next. This way, we continued for three days and four nights.

> One time, a huge wave covered the ship from stern to stem and almost filled the hold. The force was so violent that it tore the man from the helm, and ripped the whipstaff out of his hand. Although he was tossed violently from side to side, it was God's mercy that he was not broken in two. When he came up, bruised and battered, but with whipstaff in hand, unbroken, it was a cause of encouragement for all, and the passengers cheered.

> Admiral Somers cried out in a loud voice for one and all to keep

bailing. Not one man failed to serve the others in the task before us. On Thursday night, Admiral Somers saw a little round light much like a faint star. He called the others to observe as the strange light, like firelight, stayed with us for the whole night. The Bermudas are said to be enchanted and filled with witches and devils. Some of the men thought this was a tempest of evil.

To stay afloat, sailors threw over much luggage and trunks and chests. Much of the food and barrels of oil and cider were heaved over the side to try to lighten the ship. By Friday, there was great despair. After having bailed and pumped thousands of gallons of water, the poor adventurers on the *Sea Venture* were giving up hope. They were ready to commend their sinful souls to God and commit the ship to the mercy of the sea.

Reverend Bucke knelt on the deck and pleaded with God to save them from the jaws of death at the mercy of the sea and to rebuke the raging winds. No sooner had he said his Amen, than Admiral Somers cried out, "Land!" Everyone cheered and thanked God. About a half mile out from the Bermuda Islands, the ship crashed first into one rock and then another and became wedged between the two. Upright! Oh, this was not a loss but a joy, for it was low tide. All the men, women, and children safely made it to shore. They sank down on the sand with shouts of joy and many tears.

All were so relieved to have made it to land safe and sound that they did not care if a Bermuda witch was there to meet them! Ah, but it was not Devil's Island, as has been thought for so long. There the refugees fed on fish, fruits, berries, and many wild black hogs, which was a tremendous blessing since all of their provisions had been lost in the storm. (That is the only part of the story that was hard to hear, as I am still very hungry.)

Master Strachey said, "It pleased our merciful God to make even this hideous and hated place both the place of our safety and the means of our deliverance." (Hmm, I'd like God to make this hideous and hated place of James Towne my place of safety and deliverance.

51

Nonetheless, soon I will be back in England where I will eat to my heart's content.)

Master Strachey continued:

For all these months, we lived there in ease. The climate was delightful for most of the ten months, and the food was plentiful. The men cut down cedar trees of much strong wood and with cables, oak planks, and some pitch and tar—salvaged from the *Sea Venture*—we began to rebuild. We were very hopeful. We gathered every morning and evening at the ringing of the ship's bell for public prayer.

Admiral Somers launched his ship in April to see if she was seaworthy. She sailed well. Now it was just a matter of waiting for the best winds to head to Virginia. Once the ships were ready, Governor Gates set up a cross in Admiral Somers' garden. It was made of timber from our ruined ship. Next to the cross were these words:

"In memory of our great deliverance, both from a mighty storm and leak, we have set up this memorial to the honor of God. It is the spoil of an English ship of three hundred ton called the *Sea Venture*, bound with seven ships more, from which the storm divided us, to Virginia."

With the strong winds, it was less than a week's journey from Bermuda to here. Just think. They were that close to us all the time.

Oh, I am so excited, I do not know if I will sleep tonight. We had more to eat tonight. I had something called conch that is a kind of fish from Bermuda.

This is the first day I have been happy in so long. I imagine I will tell you this in person before you receive this letter.

Your friend,

Abigail

James Towne, Virginia

MAY 29, 1610

Dear Elizabeth,

Governor Gates told us that he has enough food on board the two ships to feed us for two weeks using a ration of two fish cakes per day. Of course, to those of us who have eaten acorns and dried roots every day for months, this sounds like a grand feast.

If the men find no food in two weeks, he will make ready and transport us all to England. A great cheer went up on both sides. Of course, all of us here would leave tomorrow, and I think our friends from the *Sea Venture* now know that this is not the colony they were promised.

We who have been here this last year know that it will be impossible for them to find food in this short time. Powhatan's tribes will not help the English. The fairy tale days of Princess Pocahontas bringing baskets of food are over.

Your friend,

Abigail

James Towne, Virginia

JUNE 6, 1610

Dear Elizabeth,

The James River usually has plenty of sturgeon at this time of year, but there is not a fish to be found. The men hauled their net twenty times through the river, but there was nothing. Governor Gates sent the longboat down to Point Comfort to fish, but after one week, they caught only a few fish.

It is a divine proclamation that we are to go home! I am secretly thrilled with each report of failure to find food. There is only one course left to take—abandon this godforsaken colony and go home to England!

Finally, Governor Gates decided to abandon the fort and set sail with all of the colonists in the four ships that are left—the *Discovery,* the *Virginia,* the *Deliverance,* and the *Patience.* We will head directly to Newfoundland to meet up with other English ships bound for England. I cannot wait to sail out of this dreadful place.

*Your very-ready-to-come-home
friend,*

Abigail

Mulberry Island, Virginia

JUNE 8, 1610

Dear Elizabeth,

I could not write to you yesterday. We were all so very busy. Governor Gates ordered his men to strip the houses of all possessions, pack them in barrels, and load them onto the ships. I kept Father's Bible, Mother's wedding ring, and my paper, ink, and quill pen, along with my bundle of letters to you. Soon I will deliver these letters to you in person! We languish at Mulberry Island, anchored here for the day. As soon as the tide turns, we will set sail.

The men worked all morning to load the ship while soldiers stood guard. At noon, all boarded the ship to the beating of the drum. Governor Gates and Captain George Yeardley stayed behind on shore. Captain Pierce told me that it was because of a plot to burn the fort. They can burn it to the ground for all I care.

Finally, Captain Yeardley gave a farewell salute to the abandoned fort, and we lifted anchor. I have never been so happy. Good-bye, James Towne. Good-bye, America.

Your friend,

Abigail

Chipping Camden, England

June 10, 1610

Dear Abigail,

I have not written in the last six weeks as I was ill with a fever. After I recovered, Papa was anxious to get me out of London to the good country air. When my coach arrived, Uncle met me with a twinkle in his eye.

Before I had even taken off my traveling cloak, Uncle called me down to the library. He had bought a three-times magnification telescope from a shop on the Pont Neuf in Paris! He danced around it, explaining the lenses and how they work. Uncle told me that earlier this year, the famous mathematician, Galileo, had devised a twenty-times magnification telescope and observed four moons around Jupiter!

I asked Uncle if we could see Jupiter, and his face fell. "Alas, my dear girl, we cannot. But you shall see the moon and the stars." Then he twirled me around and said, "Is this not marvelous?"

I laughed. "Yes, indeed, Uncle." Yet what is marvelous to me is that he would share the joy of this knowledge with me—a mere girl—and gladly do so. I am so blessed to be here again this summer.

Your star-gazing friend,

Elizabeth

James Towne, Virginia

JUNE 11, 1610

Dear Elizabeth,

My fortunes have changed again! This adventure continues to take such twists and turns. I know you will think me mad, but I believe God would have me stay in America. Let me tell you what has happened.

When last I wrote, we were anchored at Mulberry Island, waiting for the tide to turn. Suddenly the lookout on the *Deliverance* cried out. He had sighted a boat coming upriver toward us. It was Lord De La Warr himself with 150 men and enough provisions for a year! He ordered us all back to the fort. A few were happy, but most others—including me—were quite sad. We have been through so much during this starvation time; we just wanted to go home.

When we stepped back on shore, Lord De La Warr immediately knelt down and thanked God that he had arrived in time to save James Towne. He then strode with great authority directly to the church. There he requested that Reverend Bucke deliver a sermon. And what a sermon it was!

Reverend Bucke reminded us that if God had not sent Sir Thomas Gates from the Bermudas, we would have been out of food within a week and left to die a terrible death. If God had not directed Sir Gates to preserve the fort as we were leaving several days ago, we would not have had a fort to come back to now. If we had abandoned the fort earlier, then surely the Indians would have burned it to the ground. If we had not been delayed a few hours by the tide at Mulberry Island, we would have missed the amazing deliverance God planned for us in Lord De La Warr's arrival. If God had not directed Lord De La Warr to bring with him enough food for 400 people for a year, surely we would not be staying now.

The arm of God had done all these things. How could we fail to trust him?

I marveled at Reverend Bucke's words. My heart was stirred again as it had been when I was in England and listened to Reverend Crashaw's sermon. Perhaps God *is* in control of my life here—at James Towne—in America. Perhaps God has a reason, which I cannot see yet, for allowing me to survive the horrible time of starvation and the deaths of my parents. Perhaps God has something for me here.

After the sermon, Lord De La Warr's commission as governor for life was read to us. Then he told us of the new rules we must live under. They are tough rules, but Father always said that it would require a strong disciplinarian to make something of these weak-willed men.

Captain Pierce told me he spoke with Lord De La Warr about Temperance and I returning to England as soon as a supply ship returns. But suddenly I feel strange inside. I am not sure I want to go now. I do not feel the fear I once did about this land.

Instead, I feel strangely excited—like a new adventure is about to begin. I will keep these thoughts to myself and ponder them to see if they be of the Lord or of my own adventurous heart. At least I know this much, dear Elizabeth. My spirit of adventure has returned!

Your friend,

Abigail

James Towne, Virginia

JUNE 16, 1610

Dearest Elizabeth,

I just received the barrel you and your dear mother packed for me and sent along with Lord De La Warr's ships.

Thank you for the warm jacket. I will not need it right now, but it will be of great use to me next winter. Mistress Pierce is thrilled with the seeds you sent. I wish Mother could have lived to see them. The best of all, though, was your bundle of precious letters. I read them all in one sitting. I miss you so much. You too have a spirit of adventure. Trying to convince your father to let you study boy's subjects may be more challenging than sailing to America!

Dear Admiral Somers volunteered to return to Bermuda to obtain provisions there. He plans to bring back wild hogs, fish, and some birds. We saw him off today on the *Patience*. Governor Gates is going to return to London next month on the *Blessing* to make his report to the Virginia Company. I will send you my letters then.

Your friend,

Abigail

Chipping Camden, England

JULY 30, 1610

Dear Abigail,

You were good to put the packet of letters on the *Blessing*. Sir Thomas Gates, your new governor, and Captain Newport brought them back to England and gave them to Papa. After reading them, however, I am so surprised you were not on the ship with them. I cannot bear to read about the horrible things you have been through this last year!

Oh, my precious friend. You have been so long now in the New World. I am deeply worried over all the reports about the many troubles of James Towne. How horrid are the tales of starvation and Indian attacks. You must have been horribly frightened during that awful time. Had not Lord De La Warr arrived when he did, you might have died.

I was so grieved to hear the news of the deaths of your parents. I will miss them as much as if they were my own family for they always treated me that way.

You must feel terribly alone. Why did you choose not to return to London where Mother, Papa, and I could take care of you? I know you are a determined, adventurous girl, but it is so dangerous there with the Indians and all. What has possessed you to stay? Papa told me you refused to return to England with this ship. I do not understand. You sounded too ready to return to England.

Papa tells me there will be many supply ships to the colony this year. That means you and I will be able to send our letters more frequently. Do not forget that if you want to return to England on one of those ships, Papa told Governor Gates that you are welcome to return to us anytime. I will pray faithfully for you, dear friend. I miss your company sorely.

> With a grief-stricken heart,
> I remain,
> Faithfully your friend,
>
> *Elizabeth*

Chipping Camden, England

AUGUST 2, 1610

Dear Abigail,

I shall always remember this summer as the summer of the stars. Each night Uncle and I peer into the telescope, identify the stars, and chart the course of the constellations. I may not be able to study astronomy at university, but I am most blessed among girls to have studied the heavens at Uncle's encouragement.

I have not even minded my lessons in spinning wool thread that Mother required for my wifely education this summer. The entire time my hands are busy with the carded wool at the spindle, my mind revisits the stars I saw the night before.

What stars do you live under there in Virginia? Perhaps you could draw me a picture of what you see in the sky. I have included a copy of the chart Uncle and I drew last night of the stars overhead.

Your friend,

Elizabeth

James Towne, Virginia

OCTOBER 5, 1610

Dear Elizabeth,

There is so little time to write now. We have been rebuilding James Towne. By summer's end, we repaired the palisades, constructed a new church, and built many houses. These homes are much more durable lodgings. You would think we are turning into Indians. We built the new houses long, like the Indians do, and covered them on the outside with bark. We made mats from the marsh reeds, just like the Indians, to cover the inside of the houses. Even the youngest children help with the weaving.

You should see our church now. It rivals any cathedral in England. It is sixty feet long and thirty feet wide and made entirely out of cedar—the church, the pews, the chancel, and the pulpit. There is a communion table made of black walnut. The church has broad windows to let in the light, and two bells hang in the end of the church to call worshipers to the services.

Lord De La Warr requires fresh flowers in the church every day. That is my job, and I like my job a great deal. I take a few extra minutes when I put the flowers in the vase on the communion table to tell God what I am thinking.

Mistress Pierce and I work in the garden most of the day. We will never again have a winter like the last one. The seeds your mother sent to us are wonderful. They sprouted well, and we are growing many vegetables. We will have a feast later this year.

We planted your mother's impractical, but very beautiful, flower seeds. Mistress Pierce agreed to let me have a small corner of our garden for the flowers. She realizes that the flowers will not only encourage everyone in the church but also fill my soul with happiness. I only wish Mother were here to garden with me. She always loved to grow flowers back in England. Thank your sweet parents for me.

I am afraid I have some bad news for your mother. Her friend Mistress Rolfe died from a terrible fever. The summer here is such a sickly time. Master Rolfe is very sad, especially after they lost their poor baby girl, Bermuda, when they were stranded on that island. He spends much of his time with Reverend Bucke in prayer for mutual encouragement. I have spoken to Master Rolfe several times, and he seems quite agreeable.

Your friend,

Abigail

James Towne, Virginia

OCTOBER 10, 1610

Dear Elizabeth,

A supply ship leaves the colony tomorrow for England. I am sorry I have not written much. Those of us who made it through the starvation time work harder than anyone else. We know the importance of sufficient food and warm shelter.

Temperance returns on this ship. She begged me to go with her, but I am not ready. I told her there is more to this adventure than I have yet experienced. Temperance said, "I would think losing your parents and nearly starving to death would be adventure enough."

She is probably right, but something is keeping me here. I do not know what it is, but I sense my time in America is not yet over. I bear her no hard feelings for returning. In fact, as you predicted, I have rather come to like her. There is not much companionship for a girl my age, and I will miss her.

Please let me know if you hear anything of Admiral Somers. No one has heard from him since he left for Bermuda, and he should have been back by now.

Tell your parents that the Pierces have been very kind to me, and I am well. I know they are worried about my safety here. Captain Pierce is very brave and keeps a watchful eye on Mistress Pierce, Jane, and me. He often uses his breaks from building houses to come by the garden to make sure we are faring well.

Next week is my fourteenth birthday. It will be my first birthday as an orphan. Especially now, oh how I miss Mother and Father! Sometimes my heart feels as though it is cracking open. Then I cry until I can cry no more. I wonder if it will ever stop hurting so much.

Your friend,

Abigail

London, England

Dearest Abigail,

I just returned from the most glorious party at Middleton Hall in Warwickshire. The Cliftons were gracious hosts, and it was a wondrous affair. I wish you had been with me. I have so much to tell you, and I will not forget a single detail.

Carriages arrived all day and evening, bringing guests from London and the countryside. Sir Wentworth startled everyone by arriving from Oxfordshire in the finest coach pulled by six horses festooned with plumes. All the men were enthralled with the coach, one of the first of its kind. The tassels were silk. The curtains were the finest leather. The Wentworth coat of arms was gilded on the side of the new coach. I heard Papa tell Mother the coach cost 20 pounds! Imagine that! As much as three of the horses!

I learned that Master Shakespeare is working on a new play about the dreaded voyage and the wreck of the *Sea Venture*. Apparently, he is fascinated with the accounts of a strange glow that appeared at the ship's mast during the storm. You should ask Captain Pierce if he saw it. I wish Papa would let me attend. He says it is not proper for a girl of my status to attend the theater, but he might make an exception in this case. After all, it *is* about your grand adventure.

The day began with the men going hunting. The Middleton estate has deer, rabbits, pheasants, partridges, and pigeons, some of which we ate for dinner that evening. Papa was with the group that went hawking.

The ladies gathered in the sitting room to share news. When Mother felt the news had turned to gossip, she suggested I might want to see the library. Of course, I was quite interested in the news, but obeyed her nonetheless. And I am so glad I did. Oh, the books there! I counted them — more than 300. I could have stayed

there forever. Only when Mother interrupted me did I realize I had been reading for more than two hours.

When Mother urged me outside, I took a walk in the gardens. There were pear trees, apple trees, and cherry trees. Orchards as far as the eye could see. Papa says Sir Clifton has at least forty men who tend the gardens.

But it is Lady Clifton who should be praised. She showed Mother and me what has been filling her time this last year. Her accomplishments included building a dove house, planting one of the cherry orchards, and designing the garden in which I found myself. She confessed to me that she had also designed the chapel by relying on a copy of *Palladio's First Book of Architecture*, which she found in her husband's library. Surely if a gentlewoman such as she can build such a lovely building, a gentlewoman such as I can go to Oxford!

Alas, until I am allowed to attend that fine school, I will have to make do with talking to the gentlemen who by the fortune of birth are able to study. Many young men from Oxford College were in attendance at the party. Such learned men and so handsome.

Robert Buxton was there. You remember him, do you not? He has grown quite tall and handsome since you left. He left London for Oxford last year. He is not the young boy who used to pester us so horribly when we were younger. To the contrary, he is quite remarkably pleasant. In fact, I danced with him most of the evening.

You would have truly enjoyed him. He has become a well-mannered, winsome gentleman, worthy of further conversation, I dare say! I hope to see him again before he returns to Oxford. His delightful brother, Adam, was in attendance as well—so perfect for you! He inquired about your well-being.

I thought of you all evening—especially since today is your birthday and you are now fourteen. Do you not miss the excitement? Would you not rather be here with me, attending galas and having such wondrous experiences? How can the New World compare to the Old?

I simply do not understand why you do not return to me posthaste, dearest friend. I will continue to pray for this miracle. I miss you terribly.

Your devoted friend,

Elizabeth

London, England

Dear Abigail,

Father came home from the Council meeting where Governor Gates and Captain Newport reported such horrible events in James Towne. Lord De La Warr sent a letter to the Council stating in no uncertain terms that they must immediately send more supplies, doctors, and medicine. He said that half the remaining members of the colony have died. Do not tell me you survived only to fall ill!

Father said the Council debated whether it should simply abandon the entire Virginia venture. Governor Gates convinced them that Virginia was one of the goodliest countries under the sun, blessed with a healthful climate. Sir Gates noted that there were an amazing number of white mulberry trees — the kind needed for the production of silk. If silkworms were introduced to the colony, it is possible the product would be of better quality than that from Italy.

Father says the Company is much encouraged and interested in Bermuda as well. They have decided to raise more money for the venture. Another fleet of colonists may be arriving in just a few months! Perhaps you are truly on the verge of another adventure.

Mother admires your hard work and has been hinting that I would do well to take up some gardening myself. I would rather *read* in the garden, however, than weed the garden. I gently broached the subject again of taking additional coursework with my tutor: perhaps French or Latin? Again, Papa said no, and Mother gave me more needlework to do. I was furious. Why is Papa so stubborn about this? I wish Uncle could persuade him.

John sometimes brings home books and ciphers to work out. When he falls asleep, I borrow his books to learn what I can. If Papa found out, though, he would be very angry with me.

Your friend,

Elizabeth

James Towne, Virginia

NOVEMBER 23, 1610

Dear Elizabeth,

Henry Spelman returned! What a tale he had to tell about his adventures. His family sent him to America to become a young man of valor. Apparently, he got into some trouble in London and his family thought learning to survive in Virginia would be good for him. I am sure his family never imagined he would be traded for some Indian land!

He said he was terrified when he learned of the attack on Captain Ratcliffe. Chief Powhatan had told Henry to tell the English they could trade with him. When that trading session became a massacre, Henry was afraid for his life.

Later, he met Chief Pasptanze, chief of the Patawomekes, who came to visit Chief Powhatan. The chief showed kindness to Henry and two other English boys who lived with Henry. The boys decided they wanted to escape with Chief Pasptanze. After they had gone half a mile, one of them had a change of heart and went back and told Chief Powhatan what was happening. Chief Powhatan sent his men after them. They struck one of the boys with an ax and killed him! Terrified, Henry ran as fast as he could. Just when he thought he could run no farther, guess who showed up to help him? Pocahontas. She is real!

Pocahontas and Chief Pasptanze helped Henry to escape. He has been living with the Patawomekes far up the river from James Towne ever since. Imagine that! Pocahontas helped Henry, an English boy, to escape. Perhaps the stories about her are true after all!

Had not Captain Argall been trading in the Patawomekes' territory, Henry would be there to this day. Captain Argall first asked for the English boy he had heard was there to help in the trading. Chief Pasptanze permitted Henry to serve as an interpreter

during the trading. Before the trading was over, Captain Argall traded a large amount of copper for Henry himself!

Tonight we stayed up late listening to Henry's tales of living with the friendly Patawomekes for more than a year. During that time, he got to know Pocahontas very well. He likes her very much and says she is smart. She learned some English from Captain Smith, but Henry says he taught her even more. Henry is quite good at the Powhatan language, but the words are funny. Did you know they say *cohattayough* for summer? Tell John to try this on his schoolmates: *Wingapo!* (It means "hello.")

Many rejoiced in James Towne when they heard about Pocahontas. The old-timers in the colony who remember her visits as a young girl had always wondered what happened to her. It has been several years since they last saw her.

I, for one, think it is just fine if she stays with the Patawomekes. The Indians, with or without this princess, are not friends of ours.

We are thankful for Captain Argall's successful trading visit. Now we have a large cargo of corn, some venison, some furs — and Henry!

Your friend,

Abigail

London , England

DECEMBER 1, 1610

Dear Abigail,

Tonight I accompanied Mother and Papa to a delightful ball.
I wore my ivory damask dress with the gold bodice. Because I
am now fifteen, Mother lent me her amethyst and peridot cross
necklace and even applied a little makeup to my face. Surely she
wants me to look as eligible for marriage as possible. I did think I
looked beautiful.

There were some wonderful new young gentlemen who
caught my eye. However, I spent most of the night talking with
Temperance Flowerdew.

Temperance is relieved to be back in England. She has shared
about the awful time of starvation. You spared me many of the
details that Temperance has now told me. What a horrid, horrid
time.

Temperance is truly puzzled about why you decided to stay. I
tried to tell her you have an adventurous soul, but she said, "That
wasn't an adventure; that was a death sentence."

I cannot imagine choosing to stay in that dreary land, swatting
bugs, fingernails filthy from digging for food in a garden. You must
come home. We both miss you.

Your friend,

Elizabeth

James Towne, Virginia

December 5, 1610

Dear Elizabeth,

We have had bad news about Admiral Somers. He died in Bermuda after filling the ship with many supplies for us. His last words were to beg the men with him to take the *Patience* straightaway to Virginia. Instead, those selfish men took the ship, laden with food, for themselves.

Soon it will be Christmas. It will be nothing like the last year, except that I will read from Father's Bible. Captain and Mistress Pierce, Jane, and I are planning a grand celebration. We will have turnips and cabbages from our garden, oysters, and dried berries.

Perhaps because it soon will be Christmas, the pain of losing Mother and Father is almost unbearable. Last night I was thinking of Mother as I often do when I go to sleep. She used to brush my hair from my face when she kissed me good night. I closed my eyes and whispered, "Good night and good rest." I always picture Mother answering, "I pray God that it be so with you. God be with you."

But tonight, no matter how hard I tried, I could not remember the sound of her voice! It was like losing her all over again. I sobbed so loudly that Mistress Pierce came in to comfort me. She stayed with me until very late and held me. When she brushed the hair from my wet face, I cried all the harder. Oh, how I miss my mother.

Your friend,

Abigail

London, England

JANUARY 13, 1611

Dear Abigail,

I have wonderful news for you. Soon, three ships with supplies and several hundred able-bodied persons will set sail for Virginia.

Alexander Whitaker, a wonderful parish minister Papa knows, is coming to Virginia. Papa says you should make his acquaintance when he arrives. He told Papa that he finds his heart strangely turned toward Virginia. The reports of the Indians move him. He wants to share the good news of Jesus Christ with them. He is strong and unafraid.

Mother does not understand why he would give up such a lovely parish in the north of England for the difficulties of the New World. I think he is an adventurer like you.

I must warn you. Papa spoke to Reverend Whitaker about your need for instruction in the catechism. Papa is particularly concerned about you having no father or mother to give you proper instruction in the ways of the Christian faith. I suspect your free-spirited days may be coming to a close, dear friend.

Papa keeps a watchful eye on my education as well. I want to study so much more, but Papa is resolute. The things I am interested in are reserved for my brother. John has not one whit of interest in astronomy. He would much rather study archery or horsemanship.

John was pleased to hear the Company is sending more horses to Virginia. He told me to tell you to please not eat them.

Your friend,

Elizabeth

James Towne, Virginia

MARCH 28, 1611

Dear Elizabeth,

Lord De La Warr has set sail to London to find relief for his illness. We do not know if, or when, he will return.

We had a wonderful visit with Captain Adams of the *Blessing* this month. Do you remember the dear captain who led us through the hurricane on the way to Virginia? He still commands our ship, which is none the worse for the storm. He brought us news that Sir Thomas Dale is coming to Virginia and we will soon be under military law. The punishments are dire, so I must obey.

Best of all, Captain Adams brought me another barrel from your family. Thank you so much for the ink and paper and set of fresh quills. You do not need to worry about sending quills as geese and turkey are plentiful here, and I can make my own pens.

Mistress Pierce thanks your mother again for the abundant supply of seeds, which came at exactly the right time for planting. I see your father has sent me the *Book of Common Prayer* to study with Reverend Whitaker. I simply have no time for such study as we are in the garden from sunup to sundown. Mistress Pierce is determined to have the largest and most productive garden of all. We each must have our own plot now, so that the lazy ones will not eat unless they plant crops.

Tell John that I promise not to eat the horses, but the pig—well that is another story.

Your friend,

Abigail

James Towne, Virginia

MAY 10, 1611

Dear Elizabeth,

Today Marshal Dale arrived with several hundred new colonists! More children have come, but no girls my age have arrived. I do miss Temperance. You were right to say that I would need a friend my age. Jane is sweet, but she is so much younger than I am. I will be fifteen in the fall—almost a grown woman.

The fort is overrun right now with chickens, pigs, and cattle that came on the ships. It is a good thing we built a stable and a shelter for the cattle last year.

Sir Thomas Dale greeted Master Rolfe and introduced him to Reverend Whitaker. Reverend Whitaker seems nice enough. Reverend Bucke, Master Rolfe, and Reverend Whitaker spoke together for quite some time. I am sure Reverend Bucke is glad to have another minister here to help.

Of course, it is almost summertime, and I suppose we will again lose many to the fevers that plague our colony. Newcomers are especially vulnerable. Mistress Pierce calls it the "seasoning time." She says if you can make it through the first summer here, you likely will be strong enough to stay.

Well, I think I will stay busy and out of sight. I have no time for lessons now in church doctrine or anything else for that matter. Frankly, I do not miss it. Your hunger to study books is something I do not share. You should have been born a boy, dear friend, for the only books you will be allowed to read are fairy tales to your children one day.

Your friend,

Abigail

James Towne, Virginia

MAY 12, 1611

Dear Elizabeth,

One of the first things Marshal Dale did was to post the *Laws Divine, Moral, and Martial* in James Towne. Oh my! We are going to have to watch our tongues, our manners, and our actions. The first time a man fails to attend church services without showing good cause, he forfeits his week's allowance of food. The second time, he is whipped. The third time, he is to be shot or hanged! I suppose church attendance will be more regular now.

Marshal Dale took men from the fort here at James Towne to repair Fort Henry and Fort Charles, built by Lord De La Warr. The men left here are to cut as many trees as possible while he is away. Captain Pierce has heard rumors of a new settlement up the river.

You will soon travel to your uncle's home for the summer. What stars shall you study this year?

Your simple friend,

Abigail

London, England

Dearest Abigail,

Sir Thomas Gates is about to leave for Virginia with nine ships, many provisions, more settlers, and many soldiers to help fight the Indians. I am beginning to feel better about your situation. Now you will have both food and protection.

Papa is glad that the Company has created new interest in the James Towne colony and many more good people are willing to move to America. Sir Gates is bringing his wife and two daughters with him as well. I hope the girls will be good company for you.

I have the most dreadful news. Last night, Papa found the letter Uncle sent me with a chart of the stars he recently made. Uncle wrote that he could not wait for me to join him to study the stars again and help him with the charting as we did last summer. He sent me copies of moon maps drawn by Thomas Harriot of London. He drew them from his observations in his six times telescope in the last few years.

Overjoyed to study the moon maps, I was careless. I left them out along with Uncle's letter on a table in the parlour. Papa paced in the front hall back and forth as he decided my fate. He bellowed at Mother. He was furious with Uncle. I crouched at the top of the stairs so I could hear him, although he was so vehemently outraged, I think they could hear him all the way to Whitehall Palace.

"How impudent of my brother to undermine my authority over my daughter. It is I and I alone who will determine what will be her education. I have a substantial dowry set aside for Elizabeth, and she must find a husband worthy of it. No man is going to marry a woman who is smarter than he is. Elizabeth simply must learn her place."

Mother tried to soothe him with comments about my skills in

housewifery, but Papa was too angry. He whipped on his cloak and left, slamming the door behind him. I have no idea what he will do.

Suddenly, I remembered that I had one of John's Latin books in my room. I ran to retrieve it and put it with John's school satchel before Papa returned. I am so afraid of what Papa will do.

Your friend,

Elizabeth

James Towne, Virginia

JULY 26, 1611

Dear Elizabeth,

It is official. Marshal Dale has set aside seven acres for the first settlement upriver, about fifty miles from James Towne. He does not want everyone in one place where we all could be held captive in one fort like before. Men are working very hard to cut down enough trees and make enough lumber. They are building a cattle shed, stable, and blacksmith's forge. Others are making bricks for chimneys. Captain Pierce and Captain Tucker are building a munitions house and powder magazine to store the weapons we will need to defend ourselves.

I am sorry my letters are so short, but we are very busy. With church services twice a day and my regular duties, I fall asleep quickly at night. I will write more soon — I promise.

Your friend,

Abigail

James Towne, Virginia

AUGUST 2, 1611

Dear Elizabeth,

Governor Gates arrived today with nine ships filled with supplies! Why, there must be more than 100 cattle! I think I saw an ox as well, which should help with the plowing of the fields.

And so many soldiers! Governor Gates went to the Tower of London while he was in England. He brought back so much old armor that was just sitting on the shelves there that we have no idea where to put it. Those Indian arrows will not pierce our men now!

Oh, Elizabeth, I have such sad news. Lady Gates, the wife of the Governor, died on the trip over. Mistress Pierce told me that Governor Gates will send his two daughters back to London. I think I would have liked his girls.

I still yearn for the company of a girl my age, but one who also has a spirit of adventure. Yet I am so busy here that I probably would not have time to be a good friend. Why, look how hard it is to get a few moments to write to you!

Your friend,

Abigail

James Towne, Virginia

September 3, 1611

Dear Elizabeth,

You ask why I do not return to England. I know it must seem strange that I want to stay here now, especially after all I wrote you last year. I know our lives are very different. It is just that I know I am supposed to be here. There has to be some reason why I did not die in the awful starving time. I feel deep in my soul that I am needed here. For what, I do not know. Perhaps it is not yet time to know.

Today, as I slipped inside the church with fresh flowers, I knelt before the altar and prayed. I had Father's Bible with me and opened it to Jeremiah 29:11. "'For I know the thoughts that I think toward you,' saith the Lord, 'thoughts of peace, and not of evil, to give you an expected end.'"

Yes, I nearly died. My precious parents did die. I am an orphan in a strange land. But I know in my heart that I have a heavenly Father who has made me a promise. There are plans for a future and a hope—right here—right where I am. If I leave now, I may never know what those plans were. I simply must find out.

Your dear family has been so kind to me. There is not a ship that arrives here without some word from you, or a present from your dear parents. They have sent me clothing, seeds, writing paper and ink, and a hornbook to practice my penmanship. Please do not tell your father that I have no time to practice and am simply too tired at night to hold a book.

You, your mother, and your father have each written to me to say that your family would take me in if I returned to England. I know this is true. Ever since my dear parents died, your family has cared for me. I even had a note from John that said I could live with you if I did not eat his horse. Your family is so special to me. Only a higher call would keep me from rushing home to live with you.

I hope you can understand. It is not something I can easily explain. During quiet moments while arranging flowers for the day's church services, I know deep in my heart that I am to remain here—at least for now.

My dear friend, your last letter in this bundle caused me great concern. I know your dearest desire is to learn all you can, but perhaps you will have to wait until you are married. Perhaps you will marry a man more like your uncle than your father—a man who will encourage your learning. Do not despair. There is hope. What did your father decide to do about your uncle teaching you astronomy? I know your father was angry, but he is a good man. I am sure he will not remain angry for long.

Forever your dearest friend,

Abigail

P.S. I don't mind if you are friends with Temperance. I would have been jealous when we were younger, but she is a good friend and our link to one another. She is well acquainted with life here and can tell you all about it. I, on the other hand, am such a poor letter writer. I promise to improve.

✳ ✳

P.P.S. I must rush. The ship is due to leave soon. Guess who is returning with the ship? Master William Strachey, the great storyteller of the *Sea Venture.* You simply must meet him. You and Temperance should ask your father to invite him to visit and tell the story again. It will be better than any Shakespeare play!

London, England

SEPTEMBER 4, 1611

Dear Abigail,

I have been a terrible friend. I have not written to you since Papa found Uncle's letter and the observation charts of the stars and moon. There has been nothing to write about this summer at all, for it was as if summer never happened.

Papa refused to let me travel to Uncle's home for the summer. That is how angry he was. He would rather risk my catching the fever than have me be with my uncle. I suppose he decided education is just as bad for me as the London air.

Mother tried to convince him several times to relent and let me go. I was surprised as she has been the main source of my housewifery lessons. Nonetheless, she has a mother's heart. She could see how heartbroken I was at the news of no summer with Uncle. But Papa would not yield.

Papa engaged the services of Master Sewell for the summer and doubled my lessons in Christian doctrine. Even Master Sewell suggested some study in Latin might be beneficial for my religious instruction, but Papa firmly declined. I was not the best pupil this summer. Papa kept a close eye on my instruction and even asked to see my needlework.

The only entertainment I was permitted consisted of attending dinners with Mother and Papa. There I was to practice the art of conversation and etiquette.

It was a dreadful summer of solitude. I tell myself I must resign myself to my fate. I was born a girl and that is that. But what do I do with this yearning in my heart?

Your friend,
Elizabeth

James Towne, Virginia

SEPTEMBER 27, 1611

Dear Elizabeth,

There is much excitement here. Marshal Dale took 350 men and ships full of timber posts and planks up the James River to the new settlement called the Citie of Henricus. You should have seen the men march off in full armor. Captain Pierce just came back for more supplies. He said that in only ten days, the men had strongly impaled seven acres of ground for the town. It will be at least ten times the size of James Towne.

They are building blockhouses and watchtowers at the corners of the town. A separate storehouse for food, tools, rope, canvas, trading goods, and clothing will be placed under the control of the Cape Merchant there. Captain Pierce had to return quickly with pitch, timber, nails, and hinges from our blacksmiths.

The women and girls here have been making rush mats for the lodgings. My fingers are bloody from the work. Yet there is a spirit of excitement in the air.

The soldiers have fended off the Indians. There is a sense that this new palisades high on a bluff over the James River may survive any attack. Marshal Dale has quite an eye for defense. His many years as a soldier in the Dutch lands are surely not going to waste here.

I wonder what Henricus is like. Captain Pierce says there is a long view and fertile valley nearby. He thinks the air is healthier than here at James Towne. I wonder who will go to live at Henricus? Will Captain Pierce move our family there? I rather like it here at James Towne, but these new tales pinch my soul with adventure!

Your friend,

Abigail

London, England

November 1, 1611

Dear Abigail,

Tonight Papa and Mother went to the palace at Whitehall. King James invited many from the Virginia Company to the performance of *The Tempest*, Master Shakespeare's new play based on the *Sea Venture*!

Mother looked so beautiful in her gold brocade jacket and violet satin skirt. I helped Mother get ready, but I really wanted to be going myself. Papa remains determined to keep me away from anything that would fuel my passion for education. Mother tried to convince him this drama is entertainment, not education, and that I could practice my etiquette skills. Papa simply said, "She is not going." Mother even tried to convince Papa that there would be eligible gentlemen there for me to meet. Papa said, "She is not going to marry an Oxford or Cambridge gentlemen either."

It seems Papa not only does not want me to learn, he does not want me to marry someone who might want me to learn.

Your friend,

Elizabeth

London, England

November 6, 1611

Dear Abigail,

Your words to me are true. I have despaired for much too long now. I keep looking to Papa to see if he will change. Perhaps he never will, but it does not mean I am doomed. Hope deferred makes the heart sick, but hope again renews the heart. I must not give up. Somehow, some way I shall learn again. The stars wink at me at night as if they too know that I shall study them again.

I prayed a special prayer for you, asking the Lord to send you a special friend, one with whom you can share your adventures each day.

John wants me to thank you for the package you sent to him. He wants to know if the arrow was ever in anyone's back. Heavens above! I am sorry to even ask you, but I promised John I would.

Your friend,

Elizabeth

James Towne, Virginia

NOVEMBER 19, 1611

Dear Elizabeth,

Captain Pierce said they are building four additional forts at Henricus: Fort Charity, Mount Malady, Fort Elizabeth, and Fort Patience. Mount Malady will be our first official hospital. The builders are completing a parsonage for Reverend Whitaker just a short distance from Mount Malady and across the river from the Citie of Henricus. Captain Pierce says the land set aside for Reverend Whitaker's church (they call it a glebe farm) will be well protected right there in the middle of all those forts.

I saw Reverend Whitaker today when I placed flowers in the church. I told him I heard the parsonage was coming along nicely. Reverend Whitaker said he is going to name it Rock Hall. I must have given him a funny look, because he laughed and said, "I see you think it is an odd name."

I said, "Well, it's just that Captain Pierce told me that they are building the parsonage out of timber piles and planks and wattle and daub, not rocks."

"Ah!" replied Reverend Whitaker. "I want to name it Rock Hall because there is a verse in the Bible that is special to me. I see you have a Bible. May I?"

I held Father's Bible close to my chest. No one else has touched that Bible since Father and Mother died. Reverend Whitaker did not ask for it again. It was as if he knew—and understood.

He explained that in Matthew 16 when Jesus asked his disciples who he is, Peter answered that he was the Christ, the Son of the Living God. Reverend Whitaker was quite excited and asked me if I knew what happened next.

I was as quiet as a church mouse. I wondered what in the world this had to do with naming his parsonage Rock Hall. He continued,

"Jesus gave Simon, son of Jonah, a new name! From then on he would be called Peter."

I know my face must have shown how puzzled I was. What did this have to do with Rock Hall?

Reverend Whitaker quoted what Jesus said: "Upon this rock I will build my church; and the gates of hell will not prevail against it. I will give unto thee the keys of the kingdom of heaven; and whatever thou shalt bind on earth shalt be bound in heaven: and whatever thou shalt loose on earth shalt be loosed in heaven."

Now I was really confused. I did not understand a word Reverend Whitaker was saying about binding and loosing. It did not make a bit of sense to me, but I did not want to hurt his feelings. After all, he is so excited about being a preacher. I pretended to look sufficiently enlightened and said, "Oh, I see, Jesus wanted to build his church on a rock and so do you."

Reverend Whitaker smiled. "I know God sent me here to help others know who Jesus is." Then he paused, and added, "Especially the Indians."

Well, Elizabeth, that was that. I was not going to stand around and talk about my God being brought to the very people who killed my father and starved my mother. No, sir. I turned and ran out. I know it was rude, but I did not care. If Reverend Whitaker had been here last winter, he would never have said a thing like that.

He is a nice man, but he has a lot to learn about life in America.

Your friend,

Abigail

James Towne, Virginia

NOVEMBER 30, 1611

Dear Elizabeth,

John must be wondering about the bow and arrow. I should have written him earlier to let him know that it is a real and true Indian bow. Captain Pierce found it and gave it to me to send to John. He said that the bow is the right size for a boy John's age. It is made of locust wood and has deer sinew for the string of the bow. Tell John it is likely that an Indian boy made this bow himself using a shell to scrape the wood until it was the right size and shape. Please let John know that the arrow is real, but it missed its mark, which was a squirrel, not a person.

I have pressed some of the flowers from my garden to send to you on the next ship to London. I will also send you a quill pen I made just for you. Now you can say you have a pen made from a turkey from Virginia. It will do my heart good to know you are using the pen I made for you when you write to me.

Master Rolfe hopes a ship arrives soon from the West Indies. He is expecting some special tobacco seeds that he hopes will grow here. He thinks the climate is exactly right for them. I showed him some tobacco that grows wild in this area — the Indians use it. But Master Rolfe told me it is bitter and would never sell in London.

I must close now. The sun goes down so early this time of year. At least as winter arrives, we are not worried. My stomach is filled with turkey, goose, wild pigeon, oysters, berries, vegetables, and corn. I do miss the wondrous delicacies of cakes and tarts, though. Hmmm, are you making gingerbread this Christmas? I must not think of sweets too often. But I do miss them.

Your friend,

Abigail

London, England

Dear Abigail,

I am so glad for the spirit of Christmas. Papa has forgiven Uncle! My uncle and aunt came to visit. The first night Papa and Uncle stayed in the dining room long after supper. I longed to know what they were saying, but they closed the door to the hall. When they came out, Papa had his hand on Uncle's shoulder, and they were laughing.

Over the next few days, I looked for signs, but neither Papa nor Uncle gave any indication of whether they had talked about my education, Uncle's telescope, or my going to stay with Uncle again.

Today while Mother and I mixed gingerbread in the kitchen, I asked her about it. Mother said, "It is settled between your father and your uncle. They are brothers, you know."

That was all she would say! When I served Uncle his slice of warm gingerbread, he thanked me and commented on what a wonderful wife I would make some day. Oh, no. Did Papa convert him?

Your friend,

Elizabeth

James Towne, Virginia

FEBRUARY 3, 1612

Dear Elizabeth,

I did so miss you and your family, especially at Christmas. Please give this enclosed note of thanks and appreciation to your father for his thoughtful Christmas gift—a King James Bible. How wonderful! I will keep it with Father's Geneva Bible.

I tried to reassure your father that my training as a young Christian lady is going quite well. It is true that my training is very different from yours. Your training is formal—once a week catechism classes and special tutoring by Master Sewell. Mine just happens as I live my life here.

The church bell rings, and we all gather to pray and hear a good word from the Holy Scriptures given by either Reverend Bucke or Reverend Whitaker. They are both wonderful preachers. But I also see them every day. We talk about spiritual things while I garden or sew outside, or while I walk with them to the river. A class is not needful. I rather enjoy our talks about God. Please tell your father that things are different here but still the same, and not to worry.

You cannot imagine the changes that are taking place. In four months' time, Henricus is nearly complete. Reverend Whitaker leaves after the snow melts to live at Rock Hall. (You know, the place where people with new names get to live.)

Reverend Whitaker means well, but he cannot be serious about telling the Indians about Jesus. They will not believe it anyway. They are afraid of their god Okee. They have to make sacrifices to him so he will not be angry with them and ruin their crops. Oh well, Reverend Whitaker will figure it out soon enough.

A number of the new adventurers have asked me about Pocahontas. As if I would know! She is myth and legend from all I can tell. Old-timers speak about her in awe. They tell tales of when she would visit, carrying baskets loaded with food. If that is true,

where was she during the starving time? Certainly she was no friend to the English during that winter!

They say she used to play with the boys at the James Towne fort and turn cartwheels in the street. I think she was just a show-off. Some would like to meet her. Not me. I do not care if she is a princess of Chief Powhatan. An Indian is an Indian. She can stay away forever.

Tell your father Mistress Pierce is making sure I know my stitches. We sew many of the shirts for the soldiers who came over with Marshal Dale. He has had them working so hard that they rip through many shirts over a short period.

I have a solution for your problem of how to learn science. If you were here, you could work with Master Rolfe in his tobacco experiments! I shall convince you to move to Virginia yet!

Your friend,

Abigail

London, England

MARCH 12, 1612

Dear Abigail,

Papa came home very excited tonight. The Virginia Company received its new charter today from King James. The King will now permit the colonists in Virginia to own private land. Papa thinks that will attract new settlers.

I had not wanted to tell you this before, but Papa was concerned that many would invest in the East India Company instead. It is true that we do get a good supply of timber, potash, sassafras, and pitch from Virginia. However, many here were more interested in the exotic goods coming from East India, such as spices, silks, and indigo.

Also, fears of the Indians keep many away. Papa said some men in the Company think the James Towne venture will result in many conversions of the savages to Christianity. Others believe that the savages are devil-inspired to quench the flame of truth.

I was pleased Papa discussed these things with me. These subjects are usually reserved for his conversations with John. Perhaps he was just excited about the news. Or perhaps he thinks I would be interested as well?

Your friend,

Elizabeth

London, England

APRIL 19, 1612

Dear Abigail,

Papa relented! I may return to Uncle's home next month. If I hurry, Papa will make sure this letter accompanies Captain Argall who sails to James Towne on the *Treasurer*. I think he knows I wanted to tell you the news. I still do not know what transpired between Papa and Uncle, but I am not going to question this decision, not at all! He did not say a word about the telescope or the star charts. I did not dare ask, either.

Papa also says to tell you he has placed a chest just for you on the ship. He included a special silk dress made by our tailor. There is also a beautiful embroidered robe for formal occasions. He knows they are impractical, but he wanted to lavish a special present on you to demonstrate his and mother's high regard for you. I miss you, dear friend.

Your devoted friend,

Elizabeth

Chipping Camden, England

JULY 17, 1612

Dear Abigail,

It is a vastly different summer than I had expected. When I arrived, full of anticipation, I went straight to the library. The telescope was gone! I asked my uncle where it was, and he simply said that it was in need of repairs. Nothing more was said, then or since, about it. It is as if my last summer here never happened. I suppose Papa prevailed, and Uncle has complied.

In fact, Uncle is frequently gone this summer, and I am left with my aunt. She is a dear woman, but apart from tutoring with Master Sewell, my summer here is no different than were my days in London. I am obliged to practice the virginals, sing and play the lute for dinner guests, and sit for hours on end with Aunt as we stitch our needlework or spin the wool yarn.

I have tried my hand at making charts of the stars by viewing the night sky, but without the magnification of the telescope, the faraway lights are harder to make out.

My only solace is Uncle's library. It is a quiet and disappointing summer indeed.

Your friend,

Elizabeth

Rock Hall, Henricus, Virginia

JULY 26, 1612

Dear Elizabeth,

I received your good letters when the *Treasurer* arrived from London last month. I apologize for not writing to you sooner, but my life has been turned upside down again!

As you know, your father spoke with Governor Gates and told him that he wanted me to be instructed in catechism, the Bible, and the doctrines of the church. Governor Gates spoke with Marshal Dale, and it was decided. I had no say in it. Neither did Captain or Mistress Pierce.

It was for "the good of the colony" that I have been sent to live at Rock Hall near Henricus. I am now miles and miles away from James Towne. I am here to help Reverend Whitaker with his church in the same way I helped Reverend Bucke with our church in James Towne. Mrs. Sizemore, who is Reverend Whitaker's housekeeper, has been assigned to help me become a proper English woman.

I miss the Pierces so much. Mistress Pierce understood when I stayed up late crying about my parents. She let me sob in her arms until I had no strength. She listened to me as I told her about not being able to hear Mother's voice in my head anymore. She brushed my hair away from my face just as Mother did. And Jane was so good. She did not mind my being in her family. Captain Pierce always said that he would care for me out of the respect he held for Father.

I did not want to leave. I was so angry that I could not even put it down on paper in a letter to you. Besides, I have so much copy work to do now! My hand smarts from practicing my alphabet and copying passages from the Bible.

Please do not tell your father. I know he meant well, but I am so unhappy. I miss James Towne, the Pierces, my friends, and my garden.

Your lonely friend,

Abigail

Rock Hall

July 27, 1612

Dearest Elizabeth,

How thoughtless of me! I just poured out my troubles to you and did not even once thank you and your father for the gifts. I think your father needs to come over here and see how we live. The silk dress and robe are glorious, but I doubt I will have any occasion to wear them. Nonetheless, when I look at them, I will think of you, and how beautiful you must look when you dance the night away.

You and your family are so dear to me. Your father has always treated me like one of his own. I am most happy to be so loved by your parents (with the one exception of this campaign to make Abigail Matthews into a proper English lady).

Reverend Whitaker wrote a long letter to the Virginia Company yesterday. He asked me to copy it for my handwriting copy work so that he would have a copy of what he had said.

Reverend Whitaker urged the stockholders to care about God's kingdom here in America and not be so concerned with making a profit from our colony. He said they should care more about others, especially the Indians and their need for God, than themselves. Now I am not sure I agree concerning the Indian part, but his letter made me realize some things about myself.

You think I am brave to live this life here in Virginia. Well, I think you are wrong. After I copied what Reverend Whitaker said in his letter, I realized I am very selfish. I want everything to return to the way it was. I want to live with the Pierces. I want to live in James Towne. I want to be free and not have to learn so many proper English things (like handwriting and spelling). I want my own way.

I guess that is just pure sin—wanting what I want when I want it. I have decided to try to listen carefully in my prayer time.

Perhaps God *is* doing something here at Rock Hall. I need to stop focusing on myself and my frustration and see what he is up to. Is not that what a life of faith is all about anyway?

Your not-so-angry friend,

Abigail

London, England

Dear Abigail,

I returned to London and, alas, to my instruction with Master Sewell. Papa is no longer angry and seems content that he has established proper boundaries in my life once again.

Everyone is talking about the upcoming wedding for Princess Elizabeth. Perhaps because I have been such a dutiful daughter, Papa will permit me to go with them.

I wish you were here to go with me too. Temperance sends you her best as well. Did you know she writes Captain George Yeardley from time to time? He is a soldier there with Marshal Dale. I think he is sweet on Temperance, but Temperance thinks not.

Your friend,

Elizabeth

Rock Hall

Dear Elizabeth,

There is talk that more people in James Towne will move up the river. Maybe the Pierces will move near here, and I can see them more often. I miss them so much, but to be fair, Reverend Whitaker is wonderful to me.

He knows I was angry about having to leave the Pierce family and my friends. He told me that flowers are needful in his church as well and has given me a much larger garden than I had in James Towne. He depends on the storehouse for his grain, so he told me I did not have to plant much corn at all. Instead, he said I could plant as many flowers as my heart desired. If your kind mother would send me some seeds on the next ship, I will make good use of them in the spring.

It is beautiful here. The air is so much fresher than near the marsh in James Towne. Even the bugs did not seem to bite so much this summer. It is peaceful here at Rock Hall with plenty of land to roam.

I suppose that it also helps some that Rock Hall is miles away from James Towne where my memories of Mother and Father are stronger. Reverend Whitaker says God is giving me a new start here, and that he will take care of me. I just wish he had taken care of Mother and Father. I do miss them so.

Captain Argall stopped by on the *Treasurer* on his way to trade for corn with the Indians. I asked him when he is going to London next. He said he will be busy trading and exploring around here the next few months. It may be a while before my letters can find their way to you. I wish we could see each other. I miss you so much.

Your friend,

Abigail

Rock Hall

November 5, 1612

My Dearest Elizabeth,

How I miss you, sweet Elizabeth! I miss you more at this time as we used to celebrate our birthdays together. Mine on October 18, and yours on November 1. I imagine that a young lady of seventeen in England has a life much different from that of a young lady of sixteen in a certain Virginia colony. I bet your shoes are polished bright, while mine are worn thin and must last until the next ship. Please ask your father to send me a pair of sturdy shoes in the next shipment! No more silk dresses!

Rock Hall is my home now and Reverend Whitaker, the tender of my soul. Mrs. Sizemore, Reverend Whitaker's housekeeper, and other ladies in the church mean well, but they cannot replace my mother. They certainly try hard to tame the wildness out of me and bring me up proper. I would still much rather dig in the garden than practice my lettering or stitching.

I miss Mother. She seemed to understand my need to run free and explore and have adventures. I do not miss London much at all. I find I am in the most trouble when I have been stitching for oh, too long and all that is in me yearns to run to my garden or climb a tree for the long view. I know I am sixteen now and must abide by the rules of womanhood, but the skirts are too constricting, and perhaps the etiquette is as well.

Reverend Whitaker has undertaken to school me in all truth. I have Scripture lessons with him daily. He is quite concerned for my impetuous spirit. My anger still blazes toward the Indians — and at times, toward God. I cannot help it. His advice makes no sense to me at all. I am to trust God to take care of me, the orphan, but was it not he who made me an orphan? He forsook my mother and my father — that is certain. Now it is just me alone remaining.

Reverend Whitaker tells me I must not let this bitter root fester.

I pretend I am all done with bitter roots and have scuttled them into the compost heap. I pretend I am brave, but in the night and in my letters, I tell you what is true. I miss my parents sorely.

I will write to you again soon. Ever your admiring friend, I remain,

Faithfully yours,

Abigail

London, England

Dear Abigail,

I have such wondrous news! As a valued member of the Virginia Company, Papa was invited to attend the wedding of Princess Elizabeth to Frederick V, and we may all come! She is only fifteen, but she will be the Queen of Bohemia now. They are getting married on Valentine's Day next month. It is so delightfully romantic.

The news gets even better. You'll never guess — one of the wedding festivities is a performance of *The Tempest* at the Globe Theater! And I will attend! Papa received an invitation to accompany Sir Wriothesley, the Earl of Southampton, Shakespeare's dearest patron and friend. Papa has decided to take me with him.

Mother says I may have two new dresses. Of course, the one for the wedding must be just right. I think Mother hopes I will meet a future husband at the wedding. She is clucking and fussing with fabrics, brocades, and materials and talking with the tailor at least twice a week.

[Two days later ...] It was cold today, but not rainy, so Mother and I went shopping at the Royal Exchange. We bought fabric, buttons, and new shoes for the festivities. My dress will be a brilliant blue satin with an ivory brocade jacket. Mother has chosen an emerald green silk for her dress. This is so exciting. A royal wedding!

I must go, for Mother is calling me for another fitting. I promise to tell you every detail.

Your friend,
Elizabeth

Rock Hall

JANUARY 10, 1613

Dear Elizabeth,

Oh how I hate stitchery. I did not mind the simple sewing of James Towne. After all, we had to make shirts for our valiant soldiers. It is this fancy stitchery that frustrates me so. I find my fingers tangle up the thread before it can even reach the cloth. I am sure that your needlework is extraordinary. Mine is extraordinarily horrible. The Rock Hall church ladies who instruct me in needlework assure me that it will not always be so. Today, however, I think even they were taxed with my latest effort.

Mistress Harvey spoke of the grand reception among the men of Master Rolfe's new tobacco blend. He has been experimenting the last several years. This time, he took seeds from the West Indies and crossed them with seeds from some of his earlier tobacco experiments. There are great hopes that tobacco can become the staple crop that provides the Virginia Company with its long-awaited profit. Tell your father that the men here say Master Rolfe's tobacco is sweet and pleasant.

The church ladies spoke of how they felt safe here at Rock Hall because it is surrounded by five forts. They spoke quietly around me, but I think they were talking about Indian raids. My hands shook so badly I could not get the needle through the linen. Chills went down my back and coldness overcame me. I had felt safe here until now. I cannot bear the thought of another Indian attack.

The women spoke again of the Indian princess Pocahontas. We have heard nothing from her these last few years since the return of Henry Spelman. I prefer that the princess stay far, far away. It is just as well that no one has seen her.

I must put down my quill now, Elizabeth. My fingers are so tired from stitching that I cannot write any more tonight.

Faithfully,

Abigail

London, England

FEBRUARY 10, 1613

Dearest Abigail,

Last night, Papa and I took a boat across the River Thames to the Globe Theater to meet Sir Wriothesley. He guided us to wonderful seats, where I could see the entire stage. Just before the play began, another gentleman took his seat next to Papa and me. It was Uncle!

It turns out that Uncle arranged the entire event. He winked at me and whispered, "A telescope removed for a summer in exchange for an evening at a Shakespeare play? I trust that bargain is pleasing to you?" I squeezed Uncle's hand. Papa smiled at me. I have not been so happy in months!

In the very first scene, the ship tossed to and fro in the hurricane gale winds that seemed so real. It was hard to believe I was watching a play on a stage.

Miranda, a fifteen-year-old girl who had grown up on an island with her exiled father, said at the very end, "O wonder! How many goodly creatures are there here! How beauteous mankind is! O brave new world that has such people in it!"

You, my dearest friend, are in that brave New World with many different kinds of people. You have been hurt deeply by those different people. Perhaps the people there, the Indians, are "goodly creatures" and "beauteous." I know you must be thinking that is easy for me to say. Yet, after watching the play, I could not help but think that there is a wondrous mystery in your life there in the brave new world of Virginia that has a deeper meaning still.

Sir Henry and Uncle have known each other for years and were delighted by the surprise they had concocted for me. Sir Henry explained to me that Shakespeare had read every word Master Strachey had written in his report of the shipwreck.

You lived through that amazing hurricane, and the play brought

it so very much alive to me. I am even more in awe of how God must have his hand on you. There has been a sea change in your life these last few years with the loss of your parents, but there is something "beauteous" that is going to come out it. I just know it.

Your friend,

Elizabeth

London, England

FEBRUARY 15, 1613

Dear Abigail,

Oh, how I wish you could have been with me yesterday for the royal wedding. Fireworks exploded over the River Thames as ships gathered to salute the new couple. The royal carriage brought the princess through the streets of London so everyone could wave and wish her well on her way to Westminster Abbey for the wedding ceremony.

After the wedding, we took a boat down the River Thames to the palace for the feast and dance. Never have I seen so many beautiful maidens (and handsome gentlemen) in one place.

Papa read to me this morning from Reverend Whitaker's report, *Good News from Virginia*. Papa wants people in London to see it as Reverend Whitaker does—a great opportunity to participate in something God is doing. I told Papa I was afraid those Indian raids and the starving time did not do much for the new colony's image.

Papa seemed genuinely interested in what I had to say today. And I do not think it was just to practice my conversation skills that he asked my opinion. Then again, perhaps that is just wishful thinking on my part.

Your friend,

Elizabeth

Rock Hall

FEBRUARY 21, 1613

Dearest Elizabeth,

Reverend Whitaker and I had the discussion again. You know that he wants me to forgive those who have wronged me. He wants me to forgive the Indians for taking Mother and Father away from me. I will not!

We never seem to resolve the matter. I would rather not discuss it, but he seems determined to "get to the heart of the matter," as he says. Why will he not just leave it alone? It stirs me all up inside, Elizabeth, so much so that I will not write another word tonight.

Good night, my dear friend,

Abigail

Rock Hall

April 20, 1613

Dearest Elizabeth,

How delighted I was to get your letters. I had no idea the Company was prepared to send even more settlers to Virginia. When are they due to arrive? Will they bring a pair of boots for me?

As much as I adore the generous gifts your mother and father showered upon me, a new pair of sturdy boots would serve me well. Please do pass on to them the enclosed letter of thanks for their gifts and love.

I can hardly imagine your life now. Balls and dancing, royal weddings, Shakespearean plays at the Globe Theater, dresses of satin and brocade. It all seems so far away. My life is so different from yours. And yet, if the church ladies have their way, a proper English lady I will yet become.

Today I was schooled in my recipe book. I think this is entirely silly. I am made to copy recipes for every manner of food that is entirely unavailable in this country. We do not eat mutton or beef here. We eat wild turkey, deer, pottage stew, corn, fish, and even oysters from the river.

I know what you are thinking. You wonder how I would deign to eat oysters. You think them beneath our station, I know. But how good oysters taste though, when there are no finer delicacies to be had.

It was utter torture to copy the recipe for gingerbread. Oh, how I do miss my sweets here in this new world. I think that is the greatest hardship of all—no gingerbread!

I will have to introduce you to the finer things the New World has to offer. Perhaps you will come to visit one day. Yet, you will probably marry a fine Oxford man and then be done with your old friend, Abigail. There are Oxford men here too! Come to visit!

I will show you how to eat oysters, and you can take a special oyster stew recipe back to copy in your recipe book. Now, think it not beneath your station to consume such a delicacy of the New World!

Adventure calls here, Elizabeth. I am sure the Indians will be kinder to you than they have been to me.

Your obedient servant,

Abigail

P.S. Pray for us! News has just arrived that Pocahontas was captured by Captain Argall and brought back to James Towne. Surely Chief Powhatan will kill us all now!

Rock Hall

MAY 3, 1613

Dear Elizabeth,

I heard Reverend Whitaker talking with Marshal Dale today. It seems that a ransom demand was issued to Chief Powhatan. We will return his daughter, the princess Pocahontas, on one condition. He must return our swords and guns and seven men who were captured a while ago. We also asked for a great quantity of corn. There has been no word from Chief Powhatan.

I am not walking Reverend Whitaker's farm as I used to do. I know there are stronger forts here, but I am still very much afraid. I can hardly sleep at night. The sounds of the night are like those I used to hear outside the James Towne fort during the starving time. Are the Powhatan Indians lying in the grass waiting to attack?

Frightened,

Abigail

Rock Hall

MAY 24, 1613

Dear Elizabeth,

I am furious with Reverend Whitaker. He agreed to keep the princess Pocahontas here at Rock Hall! Marshal Dale thinks that the princess will be safer here at Rock Hall because of the fortifications surrounding Reverend Whitaker's farm. There are more soldiers here and better armor and weapons.

It does not appear that Chief Powhatan will respond to the demands any time soon, so they need a place for the princess to live and learn about God. Why? The princess Pocahontas has her own gods she can worship. Why does she need my God?

Reverend Whitaker is thrilled. I will have to take my lessons with her for he is most heartily encouraged that he finally has a savage to convert to the faith. He wants her to study Scripture right along with me! He also wants me to teach her the ways of the English. Imagine!

I am definitely not interested in what God is doing here anymore. No, sir. He can win the princess Pocahontas to himself, but he can do it without me. I told Mrs. Sizemore that I will not attend the catechism class. I do not care what Marshal Dale does to me.

In fact, I am not sure the God of the English could be God to these pagan Indians all at the same time. Not when the Indians killed my father and mother.

I am so furious. I will write no more tonight, or I may say things that I will regret. You, my dearest friend, have done nothing to deserve my ire. I doubt I will get any sleep tonight. The Indian princess arrives tomorrow.

Your friend,

Abigail

Rock Hall

MAY 25, 1613

Dear Elizabeth,

Mrs. Sizemore and some other church ladies spent the morning preparing for the arrival of Princess Pocahontas. If you ask me, they overdid it. Breads, meats, and even sweets! Mrs. Sizemore used our special spices and sugar to make gingerbread. Gingerbread for the princess! In May! Why, they are wasting our special Christmas treat on her!

Other church ladies were up early in the morning, taking the napkins off the napkin press and setting the table board for the noonday meal. Some prepared the princess's room that is right next to mine! I will keep my door locked every night. She is still an Indian!

Mrs. Sizemore directed us all in our duties and twittered about, clucking disapproval for any little thing out of place. She asked me to help, but I refused. She complained to Reverend Whitaker, but I overheard him tell her to let me be. Thank the Lord for that bit of grace. I stayed in my room and sat by the window, watching for the princess to arrive.

I tried to read my Bible, Father's Bible, but the sorrow inside nearly overwhelmed me. I miss Father and Mother so very much. My heart twisted and turned inside my chest. I may be a nearly grown woman (after all, I will be seventeen soon), but I just wish I could rest my head in Mother's lap one more time and hear her soothe away all my worries and troubles. Mother always knew exactly what to do and what to say.

Mrs. Sizemore is thrilled to meet the princess. Many have told stories about what she did to help this colony and the English, but few English are left who remember her.

I am glad Reverend Whitaker is leaving me alone now. I would much rather write to you than fuss with preparations for the beloved princess. She may have saved other lives, but she did nothing to prevent my mother from starving or my father from being killed by her people. Others may adore her. I do not.

Oh, what will I say to this Princess Pocahontas?

Your friend,

Abigail

Rock Hall

May 26, 1613

Dear Elizabeth,

Marshal Dale arrived with the princess about 1:00 in the afternoon in time for the meal. With him were Governor Gates, Reverend Bucke, Master Rolfe, and Master Hamor. To my great surprise and delight, Captain Pierce also came.

Captain Pierce seemed to know I needed him, and he stayed close beside me all afternoon. He sat with me at our meal that, thankfully, I was able to take in another room. All the important men of the colony ate with the princess. Actually, I felt a bit sorry for her having to dine with all those men and with Mrs. Sizemore clucking around tending to her every need.

Captain Pierce caught me up on all the news of Mistress Pierce and Jane. Mistress Pierce still has the best garden in the colony, but Captain Pierce says his wife hears that my garden may one day rival hers. He winked at me, as we both know that will never happen. No matter how good a gardener I become, no one can match Mistress Pierce.

I told him that I was planting figs this year, just as I had watched Mistress Pierce do. He said in all his life he has not seen two women who so greatly love to sink their hands into the warm dirt. Never did he imagine that he would have the privilege of loving them both.

When I asked him who those women were, he said, "Why Mistress Pierce and you, of course!" I blushed, for I had quite forgotten how good God was to me, providing me with such loving friends of my parents to care for me when I was distressed. Why, they have adopted me into their family and made me one of their own.

Captain Pierce said, "I know having Pocahontas here brings back painful memories. Mistress Pierce and I are praying for you.

We know that God will work much good out of this, and we believe that he has a purpose for you to be in the princess's life."

I hugged Captain Pierce tightly and several tears slid down my face. I do so miss him, Mistress Pierce, and little Jane. They had been so faithful to take me in when I was without Mother and Father. I am not sure I understand his words to me, but they were soothing. Somehow they brought comfort to my spirit. For his sake, I will try to bear this terrible burden of the princess in my life.

After their meal, the gentlemen retired to the parlor to discuss the situation with the ransom demand. Reverend Whitaker brought the princess Pocahontas to me. My heart beat very fast.

Captain Pierce kissed me on the cheek and gave me a little nudge over to where the princess stood. He then left to join the other men. The two of us stared at each other for a very long time.

Pocahontas was dressed like me. Gone were the deerskin clothes of the Indian girls. Instead, she was covered head to toe in linen — skirt, bodice, and petticoat. Were it not for her dark skin and strange cut of her hair, she could have been just any other English girl in the New World.

Reverend Whitaker said, "You should take the princess out to show her your garden." I looked at him in surprise, and said, "Outside?" Reverend Whitaker said, "The princess is to have freedom within bounds here at Rock Hall, Abigail. Surely on such a lovely day as this, and after such a long journey by ship up the James River, she would enjoy being in the sunshine with you." Well, that certainly sounded like a good idea to me. I did not want to stay inside a moment longer.

Reverend Whitaker took two straw hats down from the pegged board near the door and handed one to the princess and one to me. We looked at each other. I did not want to be with the princess, but I did want to be outside. Princess Pocahontas smiled.

I put on my hat and tied the ribbons under my chin in a bow. Pocahontas watched and copied what I did, although her bow looked more like a knot to me. Reverend Whitaker opened the door and within seconds, we were both outdoors in the sunshine, like two prisoners set free.

For a few minutes, Pocahontas just stood with her face lifted to the warm sun. She closed her eyes and seemed to bask in its warmth. Then she opened her eyes, smiled, and said, "Garden?" In English!

We walked over to my garden. I showed her my beans, squash, turnips, potatoes, and flowers. It was the flowers that seemed to interest Pocahontas most. She turned a quizzical face to me as she lifted the flower gently with her fingers. Each time, I told her what the flower was. Each time she would repeat the word. I was surprised at how quickly she learned the names.

Pocahontas squatted down and put both hands in the dirt that had been warmed by the sun. She closed her eyes again as if she were remembering something. She let the warm dirt fall between her fingers for several minutes before she tried to stand up.

When she did attempt to stand, her right foot stepped on her petticoat. She tripped and fell in the dirt. She tried to get up again, stepped on another part of her petticoat, and fell again. I tried hard not to laugh because, after all, she is a princess. But when it happened a third time, I laughed so hard I clutched my apron and wiped away the tears.

Then I realized what I had done—laughed at a princess! I probably had offended her. I looked down in horror as she sat in the dirt, and she smiled at me. Then she began to laugh too.

She reached up her hand for me to help her. I showed her how to hike up her skirts, and then I grabbed her outreached hand and helped her up. She said, "Thank you," and then haltingly added, "Abigail."

I was surprised at how well she could communicate. I had heard Reverend Whitaker tell Mrs. Sizemore that she was quite facile with our language from her time with Captain John Smith and Henry Spelman, but it still surprised me to hear it myself. She dusted herself off just as Mrs. Sizemore called for us.

Inside, I took off my hat and hung it on the peg. I helped Pocahantas with the knot she had tied. When looking in her eyes, I saw a mixture of curiosity and something else. Was it sorrow? Or maybe fear?

Mrs. Sizemore soon scuttled her off to meet the other church ladies. There was more clucking over the princess as they showed her the room, clothes, and shoes. Next came the hornbook, paper, and quill pen for school. A Bible was placed prominently next to her bed. I wondered since the princess could speak English, could she read and write it as well?

That evening Reverend Whitaker talked with Pocahontas, but Mrs. Sizemore made short order of that. "The child must get her rest, Reverend," she said sternly. Never one to cross Mrs. Sizemore, Reverend Whitaker prayed that Pocahontas would sleep well and that God would watch over her and draw her to himself.

No sooner had he said his "Amen," than Mrs. Sizemore had Pocahontas by the hand and led her off to bed. I could imagine Pocahontas being schooled by Mrs. Sizemore in nighttime rituals. I had to laugh thinking of the woman showing Pocahontas how to use a chamber pot. The church ladies now have a project—and a grand one it is. Poor Pocahontas!

So glad to be an ordinary English girl in the New World, I remain,

Your friend,

Abigail

Rock Hall

Dear Elizabeth,

Captain Adams sets sail on the *Elizabeth* in a few days and will make sure my letters get to you. I pretend the ship is named for you.

Perhaps it is a good thing Pocahontas has someone close to her age here. Reverend Whitaker tells me she is about seventeen years old. I have hardly seen her this week. The church ladies took her to visit other ladies of the colony. Probably to show her off.

They all want to have some part in turning the Indian princess into an English lady. Reverend Whitaker thinks that in several weeks the novelty will wear off and we will get back to our routine. He wants to begin our catechism lessons shortly. I am to join the class with the princess.

Reverend Whitaker thinks it will be a grand idea to invite Master Rolfe to read to the princess from the Bible. She can converse in English better than expected, but she has no knowledge of the written English word. Reverend Whitaker said he could use all the help he can get since reading God's Word for oneself is needful for a Christian. He has high hopes she will forego her heathen ways and accept the English God.

I am not so sure.

I miss you, dear Elizabeth. Soon I will have word from you as I have heard a delivery ship is due to arrive next month.

Your friend,

Abigail

Rock Hall

June 15, 1613

Dear Elizabeth,

The princess will attend church twice daily with me. On Sunday morning, we will attend church service and catechism class together. Plus there are special teachings that Reverend Whitaker gives at Marshal Dale's home every Saturday night. The princess may not participate in the monthly communion, but Reverend Whitaker wants her to watch and learn.

Even with all this instruction in the ways of God, Reverend Whitaker wants to have a special catechism class with just the princess and me. He thinks that she will feel freer to ask questions if it is just the three of us.

Today, he asked Pocahontas the names of her gods. She told him that Ahone is the creator god and Okee is the devil god. She shivered when she mentioned Okee. "Tell me about Ahone," asked Reverend Whitaker.

"Ahone is creator god. He is like sun; he gives all that is good. Okee more powerful. Okee is devil god. Okee makes us sick. Okee destroys our corn. Okee sends storms and fire to our land."

"How do you make Okee stop doing those things?" asked Reverend Whitaker.

Pocahontas just turned her head. I saw a tear slide down her cheek. She said, "Sacrifice."

Reverend Whitaker told her that the God of the English is merciful and just, loving and good. He said that nothing evil or destructive can come from him.

"Then he must be weak, like Ahone," said Pocahontas.

"Sometimes, what appears to be weak is really strong," replied Reverend Whitaker. "Sometimes what seems like defeat is really victory. I will tell you more later. For now, Pocahontas, just know that the English God is called Father by his Son, Jesus, and Jesus taught us that when we pray, we are also to call him Father."

Pocahontas seemed upset at the mention of the word "Father." When Reverend Whitaker ended the lesson, Pocahontas opened the door and went for a walk. I followed her. Pocahontas went to my garden. She knelt down in the warm dirt and sobbed. I heard her utter only one word. "Father!" she said through her tears. Did she mean Father God or her father? "Come for me," she pleaded.

I did not know what to say to her, so I quietly slipped away to let her be alone. She misses her father. I miss my father terribly. At least we share that pain.

Your confused friend,

Abigail

Chipping Camden, England

JUNE 16, 1613

Dear Abigail,

Papa rode with me in the coach from London to Uncle's home. When we arrived, Papa and Uncle had another long discussion behind closed doors. The next day, Papa left to travel back to London and carried a package Uncle gave him for safekeeping. I wondered what it was, but Papa would not say. He only told me to obey Uncle in all his requests. I thought that very strange.

We hugged goodbye, and he said he would miss my company. I believe he means that. Over the last few months, we have talked much about the Virginia colony. He has been surprised how much I understood of the true situation there. I have you, my good friend, to thank for that.

That first evening, I entertained my aunt and uncle by singing and playing the lute. Afterwards, Uncle called me into the library. I saw large sheets of drafting paper laid out on the table and ink wells and pens. Could we begin charting the stars again tonight?

I glanced over where the telescope used to be, and he sighed. "Repairs," he said, and shrugged. I suppose I had hoped against hope that Papa had softened his views.

Uncle said, "I have decided to build an orangery. And I have decided that you shall design it." He pointed to a small stack of books and turned on his heels and walked out.

I was so astonished at his request that I forgot to ask him what in the world is an orangery! I rushed out to call after Uncle, but he had already retired for the evening. I poured over the books—most on architecture, one on fruit trees from Southern Italy, but found no reference to an orangery.

The next morning, eager to find Uncle, I rose early. I joined him as he walked in the garden. I had so many questions. What is an orangery? Why does he want me to design it? What would Papa say?

Uncle said he was captivated by an orangery he had seen in Italy several months ago. He wants to import orange and lemon trees from Italy to grow in his garden. For the trees to survive our winters, he needs to build an orangery, a protected house for the trees to let in as much afternoon sunlight as possible. The trees are grown in pots, not the ground! In the summer, they move the pots outside.

Uncle asked me what kind of elements might be needful in a building like that. I thought about it for a few moments. Certainly, glass. For the sun to reach the trees in the winter, there must be many glass windows and even doors. He told me that was a good start. He told me to consider what is necessary for the trees to prosper and the design would follow. He said there is no other orangery that he knows of in England, so I am free to experiment and no one can say I did it wrong.

When I protested that I had neither the skills nor the training for this, he replied, "You are an inquisitive girl. You shall figure it out."

I argued that Papa will surely be upset. He simply said, "Your Papa has given me his authority over you for the summer. It will be fine."

I am so confused. Excited, yes, but frightened. Such a building will require great expense, and I cannot fail. I stayed up past midnight tonight thinking about it and pouring over Uncle's books—books on fruit growing, architecture, and climate in England. My head hurt when I lay down for the night, but it was a happy hurting!

Your friend,

Elizabeth

Rock Hall

JUNE 22, 1613

Dear Elizabeth,

Marshal Dale brought Reverend Whitaker a present — a horse! Reverend Whitaker has many people in his parish to visit, and Marshal Dale wanted him to be able to get around faster. He also gave us a cart for the horse to pull. This will make it easier for the three of us to attend the Saturday evening Bible classes at Marshal Dale's home.

As we admired Reverend Whitaker's fine new horse, I noticed that Pocahontas seemed at ease with the beast, even though she has never ridden one. I think growing up around so many animals puts her at ease. Reverend Whitaker thanked Marshal Dale for such a valuable gift, and asked me if I would be willing to care for the horse. We named him Admiral (after Admiral Somers) — a most commanding name for a strong, commanding horse.

Reverend Whitaker told Marshal Dale that the princess is progressing in her lessons in English reading and writing. As to her interest in the English God, he was not so sure. He told Marshal Dale that he was glad for the help of others such as Master Rolfe, who reads to her weekly from the Bible.

The princess came into the room to boldly ask Marshal Dale if there had been any news from her father, Chief Powhatan. He said there had been no response at all to their demand for a ransom for her return. The princess turned abruptly so they could not see her face. But I saw it.

I followed her to her room as she threw herself on the bed and cried. *Aha! Her father does not want her back! That is why she is so distressed*, I thought. *That is what she meant by "Father" in the garden.* She may be a princess, but she is not wanted by her own father, not more than his precious guns, weapons, and corn.

I suppose I took some pleasure in the fact that her father had abandoned her. After all, it was at her father's orders that we received no corn or help in any way and my mother starved. It was at her father's orders that my father was killed by an arrow.

I felt a little guilty, but not much. I do not think it is right to try to tell Pocahontas about our God. The Indians have their own gods. Let Pocahontas pray to Okee and Ahone now to help her.

When Marshal Dale left, I asked Reverend Whitaker, "Chief Powhatan is not going to bargain for his daughter, is he?"

"No, it does not look like he will," he answered.

"Then your project is meaningless. If Pocahontas does not go back to her tribe, then what use is it to teach her about our God? She will not be able to share it with anyone else."

"Abigail, you surprise me. You profess to know and love God, and yet you seem not to understand his heart. Do you not recall the passage in the gospel of John that says God loves the world so much that he desires not one person to perish? He said anyone who believes in him will not perish but will have everlasting life. Did God mean only the English?"

Perhaps, I thought. I will not get into this discussion again with Reverend Whitaker. We simply disagree on whether the Indians should know about our God.

He says that all men need to know of the grace and mercy of God and of the sacrifice he made for us. I say things are fine the way they are. The Indians are happy with their gods. Why, they even have two gods, not one like us. Let them be.

Elizabeth, there is a strange tugging at my heart, and I know not what it is. Reverend Whitaker says it is the Holy Spirit trying to instruct me of my own sin of bitterness and hatred of people God made in his own image. I think not. I will do what I have done in the past when this tugging comes. I will ignore it.

Your friend,

Abigail

Chipping Camden, England

July 3, 1613

Dear Abigail,

A letter arrived from Papa today with dreadful news. The Globe Theater burned down! The wondrous theater is now just ashes and rubble. A flaming cannonball shot from the cannon during a performance of *Henry VIII* landed on top of a thatched roof. The entire theater burned to the ground in only two hours. Thankfully, all escaped unharmed. I am so glad I saw *The Tempest* there just a few months ago.

Papa told me the first fire at James Towne started the same way. It was before you ever arrived. Those thatched roofs keep out the rain very well, but certainly not the fire. I must consider that in my design of the orangery.

I have been through sheets and sheets of the drafting paper Uncle left me. I have broken the nibs of so many quills. The floor is often littered with my crumpled up drawings. This task is impossible.

For the best conditions for growing citrus trees, the building must face south with lots of glass windows to capture the most beneficial winter afternoon sun. I must build something on the northern side to protect the building from severe winds and the cold. But what? Perhaps brick walls, thick ones.

Uncle and I visit the glassmaker next week so I can learn about the sizes and placement of the glass panes. Glass is terribly expensive. I simply cannot make a mistake.

Your friend,

Elizabeth

Rock Hall

JULY 5, 1613

Dear Elizabeth,

Incredible news. Chief Powhatan is willing to pay the ransom. Perhaps Pocahontas will return to her father and no longer live at Rock Hall!

I ran to give Pocahontas the good news. I found her digging in the garden — my garden. She is not supposed to dirty her hands with work like that. After all, she is royalty. The church ladies have tried these last few weeks to get that idea through her head.

Well, this will be the last day she will be in my garden. She will no longer be our hostage and will be free to return to her people.

I told the princess that her father had finally spoken. He sent back seven of the English captives. "And the weapons?" the princess inquired.

"I did not hear anything about any weapons," I replied. Her face darkened. "What is the matter, Pocahontas? You should rejoice. Your father met the demands."

"Father met part of the demands. Father will never give back your weapons."

"Do not be discouraged. Come. We will find out. I am sure he sent weapons with the men as well."

We hurried back to the parsonage where Marshal Dale, Governor Gates, and Reverend Whitaker had gathered. We heard Marshal Dale say, "This is outrageous. He sends a broken musket with each of the men. He is taunting us. We must hold her until he has paid the full ransom. She is well cared for here."

Governor Gates replied, "Ah, yes, that is what I feared. Chief Powhatan knows we will not harm her so he will simply bide his time. I agree. We cannot release her now. The idea that he does not know where the weapons are is preposterous. We must have the weapons, or Princess Pocahontas will never go home to her father."

I stole a glance at Pocahontas. She understood most of what Marshal Dale and Governor Gates said. She knew she was not going home that day. I do not know who was more disappointed—Pocahontas or me.

Reverend Whitaker said that her Bible lessons were profitable, and, with the help of Master Rolfe, her reading and writing of the English language would increase as well. "Several more months of her living here and learning of God's love for her would be more than acceptable to me," he offered.

Suddenly, Pocahontas slipped outside, hiked up her skirts, and ran as fast as the wind. She ran and ran so that I could not keep up with her. She finally came to a large oak tree with thick and strong branches. Then she scrambled up the branches, skirts and all.

She was sobbing so hard I do not think she heard me coming, even though I was breathing hard and fast from running after her. She spoke both in her native language and in English.

Her English is better than she lets on. I think she is smarter than all of us. I could understand every word she was saying. She spoke with passion and a good command of our language. I wonder why she pretends her lessons with Master Rolfe are going so slow?

She cried out that her father had abandoned her. She spoke of how she was his favorite daughter—his little Snow Feather. "Many times when my father bargained for other captives," said Pocahontas, "he gladly gave up weapons and other valuable items to redeem his warriors. Am I not as valuable to him as those men? Does my father not love me anymore?"

Her heart was breaking. She cried so loudly from the bottom of her soul that I realized she had no idea I was there. I slipped away.

I had seen part of the princess's heart that she never intended for me to see. She too loves her father very much and misses him. As I do mine. Yet her father has betrayed her.

That strange tugging is in my heart again.

Your friend,

Abigail

Chipping Camden, England

JULY 20, 1613

Dear Abigail,

Forgive me if I sound harsh. But Abigail, you are just not thinking clearly. There have been many reports here of the number of Indians the English have killed. Those dead Indians were someone's mother or father or sister or brother.

Why do you think God is only interested in being the God of the English? Where in the Bible do you read that, my friend?

Dear Abigail, *think*. What have you been taught all your life about our God? That God so loved the world he gave his only Son, Jesus, so that anyone who believed in him would not perish, but have eternal life.

Did Jesus come only to save the English? I fear your emotions will cause you great trouble there. You must think!

Concerned,

Elizabeth

Rock Hall

SEPTEMBER 4, 1613

Dear Elizabeth,

I just finished reading your letters. You too! Are you and Reverend Whitaker conspiring with one another? Now you are both quoting the same Bible passage to me. I will not hold it against you, dear friend, but I simply do not agree.

Yet, I had that strange tugging in my heart again as I read your letter. I promise I will think about what you said. Perhaps it would be best if I read that passage in the gospel of John again too. I am not changing my thinking, mind you, but I promise I will at least ponder it more.

Master Rolfe comes around more and more these days. I do not mind, though, for he often brings his friend Master Robert Sparkes. Master Sparkes talks with me while Master Rolfe reads to Pocahontas and helps her with her reading and writing from the hornbook.

I do not dare let on that I know her English speaking is much better than Master Rolfe knows. I wonder … does the princess like for him to come to see her so she pretends her lessons are going much slower than they really are? She is very clever!

Master Sparkes is nineteen, and a match for those young college men at your fancy parties. He was in the midst of his studies at Cambridge when he met Reverend Whitaker and decided to come to the New World. Reverend Whitaker encouraged him to finish his university training first, but Master Sparkes had too much adventure in him to stay in England.

He likes to visit Reverend Whitaker's parsonage, though, and look through his library. Reverend Whitaker walks around whistling for weeks after he gets a package from his father or his brother, Jabez. His package is always full of books, and he lets Master Sparkes borrow them.

Master Sparkes has blond hair and blue eyes that sparkle when he laughs. He has decided to help Master Rolfe with this next crop of tobacco. He says Master Rolfe is one of the hardest workers he has ever known.

Master Rolfe is determined to keep up his experiments until he finds the right blend of seeds and the best process for curing the tobacco leaves. He wants a crop that will cause London to be thankful it has a colony in America.

Have you heard anything about the first crop he sent over this summer? Would you ask your father? This supply ship brought no news about his tobacco. That is unfortunate, because Master Rolfe is at work harvesting his next crop even now.

Today, after our lessons, we went to Master Rolfe's fields. Reverend Whitaker offered us his horse, while Mrs. Sizemore clucked her disapproval. She would much rather have us work on our needlework with her church ladies.

Of course, Pocahontas and I are always happy when we are outside. The princess knows much about tobacco, at least the Indian kind. Master Rolfe says it is much too bitter for the English taste, but he is interested in what Pocahontas knows about growing tobacco in Virginia soil.

The princess spent many hours in his fields moving among his tobacco plants. She carefully examined the plants and the coloring of the leaves. She felt the leaves between her fingers, crushed some of the leaves, and then smelled the aroma they released. Sometimes she would crush the tobacco leaves and smell them while her eyes were closed and her face was lifted to the warming sun.

Master Sparkes explained to me that knowing when to harvest is equally as important as what kind of tobacco seeds to plant. Harvesting plants too early or too late can ruin the crop. The princess smiled at Master Rolfe and said in her best English, "It is time."

Master Sparkes said he would escort us back to the parsonage, but we assured him we could make it back ourselves. Besides, both

Pocahontas and I knew what we wanted to do. We wanted to see how fast Admiral could run.

We both sat on Admiral in our most ladylike manner, side saddle, skirts pulled up modestly covering our legs, the way an English lady rides. We gently prodded Admiral to walk slowly down the road as we waved—oh, so ladylike—to Master Rolfe and Master Sparkes. Then, as soon as we were out of their sight, we straddled Admiral, kicked his sides, and hung on for dear life.

Admiral seemed to sense our need for freedom and ran like the wind. We leaned low over Admiral's neck and clung to the reins and his mane. It was glorious! Both Pocahontas and I laughed with joy as we rode back to the parsonage. A few miles before the parsonage, we slowed down and walked Admiral the rest of the way home so he could cool down.

We were quiet for a while. Then Pocahontas said, "I know that you do not like me. I do not know why." She let the sentence hang in the air. It was more a statement than a question and yet, I knew she deserved an answer. But was this the time?

I could not decide whether to answer her or not. I spent so much time thinking about it that I was surprised to realize we were back at Rock Hall. Pocahontas slipped off Admiral and went inside the parsonage. I dismounted and took Admiral's reins and walked him to the barn.

The entire time I brushed Admiral, I could not stop thinking about what Pocahontas had said. I put Admiral's blanket on him, gave him water, and then closed the stall gate.

Pocahontas sat quietly in the library all evening while Reverend Whitaker read to her from the Bible. I felt too guilty to be in the same room with her and went to bed early.

Elizabeth, I do not know what to say to her. I still do not like her. She knows it, and I know it.

Your troubled friend,

Abigail

Chipping Camden, England

September 7, 1613

Dear Abigail,

It is finished! My design was approved by Uncle, and he immediately hired the artisans needed to build the orangery. Some of them laugh at the idea. They have never heard of a glass building for growing trees indoors in pots!

Uncle told Papa he needed my help, and Papa gave me special permission to stay here until late autumn. I wonder if Papa knows what I am doing. When I ask Uncle, he just flicks his hand and changes the subject. He probably does not want to make Papa angry either.

Uncle ordered orange, lemon, and citron trees from Southern Italy. They will arrive in two months' time, so we best have the orangery built by then! Uncle says that as the architect, I will need to supervise the construction of the building.

The orangery will be ten-by-eight feet, about the size of Uncle's buttery. The glass windows will sit firmly in low brick walls on the southern, eastern, and western sides. The glass panes will be blown by hand by the most wonderful artisan who is able to make them very large, some four-by-six inches. There will be a door in the eastern exposure to bring the pots outside in the summertime. Wooden shutters will protect the glass at night from the cold.

The northern wall will be solid brick, with four bricks across to provide extra protection. Although the thatched roof would provide the most warmth, I decided in favor of clay tiles with straw underneath for insulation. It is more expensive, but Uncle agreed. From time to time we may have a small fire in the orangery for added warmth so the tiles are the better choice.

The workers arrive tomorrow, and we will begin to build!

Your friend,
Elizabeth

London, England

SEPTEMBER 29, 1613

Dear Abigail,

Uncle and I came to London to visit my family for a few days. Uncle wants to purchase hinges for the glass door here. The brick masons are laying the brick walls to my specifications while we are gone.

London finally has fresh drinking water! At the opening ceremony, Lord Mayor Thomas Middleton turned the wheel at the reservoir and cried out, "Flow forth, precious spring!"

It has taken four years to build, but now a channel of aqueducts takes pure water from Hertfordshire and moves it across forty miles and one hundred wooden bridges as it dips and winds its way to London. Once the water gets to Clerkenwell, it pours into pipes made of hollowed elm trees and is piped into different parts of London. Clean water comes directly to our homes!

No longer will we have to buy our water from the Honorable Company of Water Tankard Bearers who Papa says always overcharged. No longer will our water be polluted. I cannot wait to taste the clean, fresh water that will come right into the cistern at our home.

I have never asked you how you get your water in Virginia. I assume you have no Honorable Company of Water Tankard Bearers to bring water to your home. What do you do? Sometimes, I forget that you are worlds away with a very different life.

Your friend,

Elizabeth

Rock Hall

OCTOBER 6, 1613

Dear Elizabeth,

We did not see much of either Master Rolfe or Master Sparkes during September. They were busy harvesting Master Rolfe's tobacco crop. The tobacco leaves are curing under hay now. Pocahontas suggested Master Rolfe dry the leaves hung over sticks rather than leave them in heaps on the ground. He is not sure about this method, but is trying it.

He seems to respect her and the ways of her people. He does not seem to hold any grudges against the Indians. In fact, he seems to have a respect for Pocahontas's knowledge of agriculture—a respect he gives to her despite the fact that she is a woman.

I think he is sweet on Pocahontas. They see each other at church and at Saturday night Bible studies. He also comes by our catechism classes on Sunday afternoons. But it is the simple reading and writing sessions he has with Pocahontas nearly every week that betray his feelings. I am sure he likes her.

I told Robert—I mean Master Sparkes—what I thought. He told me to say nothing of this to the princess. He added, "It is true that Master Rolfe has found a grace and love in his heart extended toward the princess, but he would never want her decision about God to be clouded by any other emotion or feeling. He wants her to study the Scriptures, learn about God's love for her, and respond to that first. He is a man of great honor. He wants nothing more than the best for Princess Pocahontas. In his mind, the best is for her to find the love of God in her own way."

I assured Robert I would not say anything. Besides, the more Master Rolfe comes to visit Pocahontas, the more likely it is that Robert will come to visit me. Those two seem to go everywhere together. Robert is learning all about tobacco growing from Master Rolfe, and Master Rolfe has called him a very quick learner.

It is Master Rolfe's hope that tobacco will become the crop the colony so desperately needs to make London and the Company take notice of the Virginia colony. So much attention in London has turned to Bermuda where there are no deadly Indians or diseases to deal with. Master Rolfe is afraid that if a valuable crop is not found soon, the stockholders will cease to care about Virginia.

What have you heard? Are the stockholders still willing to help us?

Your friend,

Abigail

London, England

Dear Abigail,

When we returned to Chipping Camden, the brick foundation and the walls of the orangery were nearly done. I checked the completed walls against the measurements in my plan, and they are perfect. I had no idea that disaster was just around the corner.

For the last several weeks, the metalworkers framed the window walls. It was slow going. Each opening for a window is set in a rectangular lead frame. Then, the lead frames are soldered together. Although Uncle told me I was to supervise the workers, I had no idea what they were doing. I finally just left them alone to do their work.

One night, right before sunset, I checked on the pallets of beautifully crafted rectangular windows that were stacked and covered at the south end of the site. I was so excited. Soon each one of these single lead grids would hold a brilliant pane of glass, and walls of windows would soar to the sky! I admired my design as the sun glinted off the metal.

An hour later, a storm arose with a fierce gale. I stood at the window of Uncle's home, watching the storm, when suddenly, the metal grid twisted in the wind and ripped from the brick foundation! It crashed onto the pallet, shattering *hundreds* of panes of glass.

I raced out to the orangery. The remaining metal grid, twisted and useless, lay across the brick wall. Thousands of pieces of broken glass were scattered all over the lawn. Weeks of work—gone in an instant!

I fell on my knees and sobbed. Uncle had trusted me with the design and invested vast sums of money in this building—especially the glass panes. Now it is ruined.

Who do I think I am? Papa is right. I am a girl, and girls do not design buildings. Oh, how can I face dear Uncle with this news? He believed in me.

Your friend,

Elizabeth

Rock Hall

OCTOBER 17, 1613

Dear Elizabeth,

Tonight we had a ball of our own—a harvest ball. The squash and pumpkins have grown large this year. The men shot a record number of deer, and the meat has been stripped, roasted, and salted. We crossed the river to the Citie of Henricus in our boat. The Citie was lit with bonfires (but not too near the thatched roofs!).

People were having fun everywhere I looked. Men bowled in the streets. Musicians played flutes and strummed lutes. Everyone sang and danced. Piles of food strained the table boards. Most of it was soon eaten by the merrymakers.

The colonists paid a great deal of attention to Pocahontas. She was dressed in regal fashion. Mrs. Sizemore had seen to that. While I was dressed in plain linen, Pocahontas stood out in royal blue silk. She looked every inch a princess, but not very comfortable.

Both Robert and Master Rolfe were present. Master Rolfe spent most of the evening with Marshal Dale and Governor Gates, but he watched the princess. He did not dance with her once.

Fortunately for me, Robert did not need to worry about appearances. He danced the night away with me. I had a glorious time. I suppose the dancing shoes your Papa sent for my birthday were not so silly after all.

When we arrived home at Rock Hall, we were tired, but not sleepy. Mrs. Sizemore clucked about us needing our beauty sleep, but we wanted to stay up. Reverend Whitaker served us mugs of warm apple cider, and we talked and laughed about the evening. Reverend Whitaker seemed pleased that Pocahontas had such a good time.

He then excused himself and left the two of us alone. Pocahontas looked at me. I looked at the fire. I have tried to avoid being alone with her since the day she asked me why I did not like her.

We were quiet for a few minutes. There was no sound but the crackling of the fire in the fireplace. Pocahontas stared at me. I knew the question she was going to ask before she asked it. "Abigail, you must tell me now. Why do you not like me?"

Yes. It was time. Seeing all that food tonight reminded me of another fall when there was no corn, no food, and absolutely no hope.

"Pocahontas, your father is head of all the Indian tribes in this area. He has much power. He can use it for good or for evil. Four years ago, I lived in James Towne with my father and mother. We came over on a ship from England to start a new life here in America. That year there was very little food."

"Go on," Pocahontas said.

"Your people would not trade with the English settlers. Your people kept the corn to themselves and would not help us. Your people watched and waited until we were so hungry we came out of the fort to fish or hunt or gather food. Then they would shoot us with arrows."

Pocahontas sat quietly and listened intently.

I continued, "Each of us had a small ration of food every day. My mother was very sick. I did not know it for a long time, but she would put part of her ration in with mine every day. Soon she was starving to death. Her body got weaker and weaker. Father felt he had to do something." I gulped.

"What happened?" she asked, barely above a whisper.

"He went out at night to forage for berries or root vegetables—anything to help Mother. One night he was shot to death by an Indian arrow. Mother lost consciousness and died a few days later, never knowing that my father had died before her."

We sat very still for a long time. I had simply told the facts of what had happened four years before. Finally, Princess Pocahontas stood and said, "Thank you. Now I understand." She went up the stairs to her bedroom.

I stayed in my chair and stared at the fire while the embers died down. The tears that had been pent up for so long began to flow, and I did not try to stop them. It felt so good to cry. The pain of the hatred I have carried in my heart seemed to pour out as well. I cried until tears came no more. Then I too went to bed.

Your tired friend,

Abigail

London, England

OCTOBER 20, 1613

Dear Abigail,

I have never been so miserable. Uncle was kind enough, but I could see his furrowed brow. He too was wondering how in the world we could start over from here. Those panes of glass are very expensive, and the metal grid is unsalvageable. He has not said much. I feel simply awful.

I keep going over it in my mind. What went wrong? I must put it out of my mind because I know this is the end of the orangery.

Your friend,

Elizabeth

London, England

Dear Abigail,

I was right. It is over. Uncle sent me home. We never really talked about it. He was not angry, but disappointed. No more disappointed, however, than I am in myself.

I do not think Papa knows anything. He has not said a word about the orangery. Just as well.

Yesterday, our family went to the Lord Mayor's show. This year it is called *The Triumphs of Truth*. The entire time, I thought, *There is no triumph in the truth I have discovered about myself—I am not as bright as I thought I was.*

For John's sake, I pretended to enjoy the show. Because of Papa's friendship with the Right Honorable Lord Mayor, we rode on one of the barges down the River Thames to Westminster Abbey to see the Lord Mayor take the oath of office. All along the way were splendid scenes erected on river barges by the guildsmen. Of course, because the guildsmen are true craftsmen (and not a pretender as I am), their designs all held up well.

The only time I was truly happy yesterday was when I watched the pageant of Robin Hood and his green huntsmen complete with their bows and arrows. They enlisted John as one of the Merry Men! He proudly carried the Indian bow you sent him.

Papa says I must hurry and finish. Another ship leaves soon for America, and he wants to put my letters in the barrel Mother packed for you. There is a surprise for your birthday.

Your friend,

Elizabeth

Rock Hall

October 30, 1613

Dear Elizabeth,

Today we had another handwriting class with Reverend Whitaker. He had us copy the Lord's Prayer over and over again until we had a perfect copy. Our hands were sore, and our quill pens were no longer sharp enough to write.

Thankfully, we were excused this afternoon. We went straight to the garden to gather pumpkins and squash. There is such a grand harvest this year, and there are still pumpkins on the vine to pick.

Afterwards, I showed Pocahontas how to bake a squash pie. We chopped up the squash and a few onions, added some ginger, and then piled the mixture into the pastry. We put the pie pans in the oven under Mrs. Sizemore's watchful eye. It was too glorious a day to stay inside any longer, so we begged Mrs. Sizemore to watch our pies for us and take them out of the oven when they were ready.

We whipped off our aprons and ran down to the barn to saddle up Admiral for a long ride. The leaves are golden and glorious red. The warmth of the sun is just right for this time of year.

We stopped along a stream for Admiral to get a drink of water. Pocahontas jumped off Admiral's back and ran to the stream. She watched the otters playing and made high-pitched screeching noises just like the otters. I laughed, but it made the otters sit up and take notice. A few of them came closer to Pocahontas.

I tied Admiral to a tree and sat down beside Pocahontas. Robert had told me a story about the princess that I could not believe was true, so I decided to ask her myself. "Master Sparkes tells me you have saved the English from certain death more than once. He said that you even offered your life for Captain Smith's. Is that true?"

Pocahontas smiled. "John Smith was a good man. He was my elder brother."

"Your elder brother?" I repeated.

"Many years ago, Captain John Smith was captured by my people. The tribe prepared a grand feast to celebrate the execution of the captive English warrior that night. After the feast, two warriors in our tribe brought two large stones before my father. They took them over to Captain Smith and forced his head down on the two stones. The mighty warriors raised their clubs to smash his head."

"How horrible!"

"I ran over to him and put my body between Captain Smith and the Powhatan warriors. I placed my head on his. If anyone would die that night, it would be me, not Captain Smith."

"What happened then?"

"My father, the great chief, was surprised, for it is only once in my life as a princess that I am permitted to make this sacrifice. Why I chose to do it then for this English warrior, he could not understand. But it was done. Chief Powhatan spared the life of Captain Smith, and he was adopted into our tribe. Because I gave my life for his, he became my elder brother."

I had no idea that Pocahontas had done this for Captain Smith. She was only ten years old at the time! How could someone so young be so brave and resourceful?

Pocahontas continued, "Captain Smith was always very kind to me. I did not want to see the English die. For many months before this happened, I carried baskets of food to the colonists. When I was captured and brought to James Towne, I saw Sam Collier, all grown up now too. He and I used to spin cartwheels together through the streets of the town."

The silence hung heavy. Finally, I asked, "If you brought the English corn in 1607, why did you not bring it again two years later when we were starving?"

Pocahontas chose her words carefully. "There was a terrible drought that summer. The corn did not grow as we had hoped. Many stalks of corn did not get higher than a few feet. We had very little supply for our people and none to share. Corn and roots were rationed. Even good spring water was scarce. Many in my tribe died as well."

I looked at my hands, sensing there was more to the story.

"But mostly," she said, "I was afraid of my father. He gave me strict orders not to help the English anymore. Earlier that year, I learned that my father was planning to invite Captain Smith and his company to a banquet, then kill them all afterward. I warned Captain Smith of the plot. I did not know then whether to return home or move on because defying my father meant the end of my relationship with him. He would rightly question whether my loyalty fell to him or the English."

"Then why did you do it?" I asked.

"The truth was that my loyalty was to Captain Smith. When he was severely wounded and sent back to England to die, I did not know what to do. I had committed an act of treason. Though we never spoke of it, my father knew that I had warned Captain Smith. I did not dare cross him again. What good would it do, anyway? We would not have had enough food for all the English — so many of you — in the year of the drought."

"Couldn't you have tried to save some?" I demanded.

"I didn't know how. Captain Smith could negotiate with some of the other tribes. The men left in charge after his deathly wound could not. They only made things worse. I knew no one I could have spoken with that I could trust. Not like Captain Smith."

"My father was one you could have trusted," I told her.

Pocahontas replied gently, "Yes, perhaps if I had known him. Perhaps, if he were like you. But I knew no one else. I had chosen the English with my actions, first in saving Captain Smith and then in warning him. Now that he was gone, I had to choose my father. He would not have hesitated to banish me from his sight if I had disobeyed. He no longer trusted me and had his warriors keep a close watch on me at all times. He let it be known to all that if I made contact with the English, then I would be executed."

"His own *daughter*?" I cried.

"I do not agree with my father," Pocahontas cried. "I want there to be peace between our peoples. Both of our peoples have killed those who are innocent. Your mother and father. My aunt and her children. This awful war between us must stop, but it cannot as long as we are suspicious of each other."

"I suppose you think you and I should be friends—for the good of our two peoples," I said. I was angry at the thought.

"It would be a start," replied Pocahontas.

Pocahontas gave me much to think about as we rode home. Home. Come to think of it, we are both away from what home used to mean to us. We are now both, through no choice of our own, at a home called Rock Hall across the river from Henricus and miles from James Towne. This is home now. Home without mother or father. Home without choice. Home nonetheless.

Never was I so glad to see Reverend Whitaker and Mrs. Sizemore. Even her clucking did not bother me, as she proudly placed our squash pie on the table board for supper.

Much to think about.

Your friend,

Abigail

Rock Hall

Dear Elizabeth,

We continue our lessons faithfully each day. I asked Pocahontas why she does not let Reverend Whitaker and Master Rolfe know she speaks, reads, and writes English much better than they think she does. She began to read and write English words with Captain Smith years ago. He had written down many words in her language and shown her how to write the English word as well.

Pocahontas says that Reverend Whitaker and Master Rolfe both get such pleasure from her every accomplishment, she cannot deny them that joy. She showed me how Reverend Whitaker's face lights up when he realizes she has understood a new idea. I laughed at her impression of Reverend Whitaker. He does so love it when we understand his teaching.

Then, Pocahontas said something rather strange. "Actually, I need time to think and consider this God of yours. It confuses me. I need time for my spirit to understand what my mind is learning. If I slow down the 'mind' learning, then the 'spirit' learning can keep up. I give much thought to the things Reverend Whitaker is teaching us. They tug at my heart."

I was shocked. Pocahontas said they tugged at her heart. That is what happens to me too, but I know what it is. It is the Holy Spirit urging me to the truth. Sometimes I do not want to pay attention, but I know that is what it is. I wonder if the Holy Spirit is at work in Pocahontas's heart now to urge her to the truth.

I have to close now. I need to feed Admiral. I let it get much too late so that I could finish my letter to you. I must hurry or Reverend Whitaker will be cross with me.

I will write some more tomorrow.

Your friend,
Abigail

Rock Hall

November 10, 1613

Dear Elizabeth,

After I finished my letter to you nearly a week ago now, I put down my quill. I took my candle to the fire to light it and, holding it aloft in my hand, I made my way to the barn. It was very cold, but I knew I would only be there for a few minutes so I did not wear my jacket. I put the candle on the niche in the wall of the barn. Admiral was skittish. I told him, "Whoa, boy. It is okay. It is just me, Abigail, with some food."

His ears were back and his eyes were ablaze. Then I saw what he saw — a snake coiled in the hay very near to me!

I did not move a muscle while I tried to think of what to do. Admiral neighed louder and become more frightened. I tried to calm him down, but I was terrified myself. I had one eye on Admiral and the other on the snake.

"Whoa, boy," I said over and over. I reached up to put the halter over his head so I could lead him out of the stall. Then Admiral reared up and pawed at the stall and me!

I was so surprised that I did not notice that he had knocked down the candle into the hay. The hay on the barn floor caught fire. Just then the snake decided to strike. It bit my ankle! It hurt so much as the poison spread. The snake slithered away, but I began to feel faint.

I had to get out of the barn, but I would not leave Admiral. There are only six horses in the entire colony, and we could not lose Admiral. I limped over to him to try to get the halter on him again. He was even more skittish now that the flames were licking the sides of his stall. He railed up again, and this time he knocked me down. My head hit the gate to his stall, and I fell to the ground.

All would have been lost but for Pocahontas. She heard the terrified whinnies of Admiral and knew immediately that something was wrong. She raced down the stairs and out to the barn. Despite the flames, she rushed into the barn, grabbed Admiral's halter, and quickly put it on him.

She helped me up and somehow got me on Admiral's back. Then she jumped on his back as well. Pocahontas rode Admiral through the flames into the yard.

By that time, Reverend Whitaker and Mrs. Sizemore had rushed outside as well. The three of them watched as the barn burned to the ground in a matter of minutes.

Reverend Whitaker carried me inside and gently placed me on my bed. Mrs. Sizemore then saw my ankle. It was burning red to the touch and puffed out twice its size. Alarmed, she looked at Reverend Whitaker. I knew that a poisonous snakebite could kill a person in just a few hours.

Pocahontas said, "I know what to do." Relieved, they stepped aside but were shocked when she returned from the kitchen with a knife. She cut open the bite wound. Over and over, she sucked the venom from the wound and spit it on the floor.

Mrs. Sizemore nearly fainted. If it had not been for Pocahontas's quick work, the poison would have spread to my heart and killed me.

I owe my life to the girl I had determined from the beginning to hate.

Your very-glad-to-be alive friend,

Abigail

Rock Hall

November 12, 1613

Dear Elizabeth,

Reverend Whitaker teaches Pocahontas her lessons alone while I recover. Mrs. Sizemore keeps my snakebite wound covered in lemon balm that is prescribed in *The Herbal*. Pocahontas says it is a good thing Mistress Pierce taught me to garden, for my dried herbs are exactly what is needed to pull the venomous poison from the wound.

Mrs. Sizemore fusses over me, clucking as she goes, but I must admit that I am thankful for her attentions. Pocahontas and I cannot stop laughing when we remember the look on Mrs. Sizemore's face when she saw Pocahontas spitting on the floor. So much for the royal princess lessons!

After her lessons with Reverend Whitaker, Pocahontas visits me, and we talk about what she is learning. Today they talked about the need for a sacrifice to pay the penalty of sin. It caused Pocahontas great distress, and I asked her why.

I was horrified to find out that her people sacrifice children to Okee, their devil god. If there is a big storm, a terrible drought, or a long sickness, the priests call for the sacrifice of a child to appease this devil god.

Can you imagine? They believe that if they kill a child, this devil god will go away and leave them alone for a while. The awful thing is that he is never satisfied. Can you imagine growing up wondering if you would be the next child sacrificed to the devil god?

I tried to explain to Pocahontas what Christians believe. Yes, it is true that God said there must be a sacrifice of life to deal with sin once and for all. The difference is that God sent his child to take on the penalty of our sins and be killed in our place. The sacrifice required by God was fulfilled by God. Only a pure sacrifice—God's only Son who never sinned—could be sufficient to deal with the penalty of sin once and for all.

Pocahontas asked if there were ever any more sacrifices after Jesus died. "No, because there was no need." She seemed puzzled so I explained, "When Jesus died, God did not leave him in the grave. He resurrected him—made him live again—three days later. Then, God told us that the only requirement after what Jesus did—dying in our place—was to believe that he did this as a way for us to be right with God."

"Reverend Whitaker said that God redeemed me with this sacrifice."

"Yes," I agreed. "Remember when you redeemed Captain Smith's life with the offering of your own that night? Well, God has redeemed *your* life with the offering of his own life—his own Son's life. That was the last needed child sacrifice. The sacrifice of God's own Son because he loves you and me so much."

"But all I have to do is believe this? No more sacrifice?"

I told her that I know it seems strange, but this is exactly what Reverend Whitaker means when he says we are saved by grace. It means we are saved because of what God does, not because of what we do.

"When you saved Captain Smith, did Chief Powhatan change his order to kill Captain Smith because of anything the captain did? No, it was because the chief was pleased with your sacrifice. You offered your life for Captain Smith's, and that sacrifice redeemed his life."

Pocahontas nodded slowly.

"Now imagine that what you did was done for every man, woman, and child for all of time in one act. Jesus offered up his life as a sacrifice. We know God was pleased with that sacrifice, because he raised Jesus from the dead. He is now our elder brother, Pocahontas, if we will accept what he did to redeem us."

"And I do nothing at all?" she asked, doubt in her voice.

"I know this may sound strange, but what if Captain Smith had not chosen to let you redeem him from your father's wrath? What if, instead of lying there quietly as you placed your body over his,

Captain Smith got up to try to fight for his own life. What do you think would have happened?"

"Why, he would surely have been killed," Pocahontas said.

"That is exactly why we must accept what Jesus has already done for all of us, Pocahontas. You can try to please God on your own, or you can trust in the Redeemer's work for you."

Pocahontas sighed deeply. "Some of what you say does make sense to me. Something continues to tug on my heart, and I will not rest until I fully understand."

Elizabeth, you and Reverend Whitaker are right. I had such a bitterness of soul over the loss of my parents, I could not see what God wanted to do right here at Rock Hall. He let a special person come to live here so she could learn about him. I was so angry at what happened to my parents that I almost missed the chance to be her friend.

If Pocahontas decides to accept the sacrifice of Jesus, it will be with all her heart, her soul, her mind, and her spirit. She will not make this decision lightly. I think she realizes that this will keep her from being with her father ever again.

We must pray for her.

Your snakebitten but very happy friend,

Abigail

Chipping Camden, England

NOVEMBER 20, 1613

Dear Abigail,

I am back at Uncle's home! Papa came in one morning and said Uncle needed me. He would not explain why, but the next day I was in the coach on my way to Chipping Camden. When I arrived, Uncle hurried me outside behind the house. I could not believe my eyes. There in a neat stack were hundreds of new glass panes. Uncle smiled gleefully, and said, "We begin again!"

I have been in the library for three days straight reading everything I can find on buildings, framing, and design. There must be a reason the other design was not strong enough.

I will not disappoint Uncle again.

Your friend,

Elizabeth

Rock Hall

November 23, 1613

Dear Elizabeth,

Master Rolfe visits Rock Hall at least twice a week now. This, of course, is in addition to our daily church services, our Sunday afternoon catechism class, and Marshal Dale's Saturday evening teachings. Robert joins him as often as possible.

Robert has asked Reverend Whitaker if he might court me, to which Reverend Whitaker gave a resounding no — at least not until I am eighteen, he added with a wink. Court me? I like Robert. I do. But courting for marriage? In just eleven months time? I am definitely not ready for that! But perhaps some day...

Today both gentlemen stayed for dinner and for a long game of Nine Pins Morris. It was great fun.

Pocahontas is very mischievous. She knew that all three men — Master Rolfe, Robert, and Reverend Whitaker — love their English education and prefer to think of themselves as university men. Pocahontas presented a play for them on the education of women in the colony of Virginia.

She borrowed Reverend Whitaker's reading spectacles and perched them on her nose. She then read from the Bible with her loudest voice, as if she were preaching from the pulpit at the church. She called on each of the men with questions about the Bible passage she had just read, but she would not let any of them answer before she was on to her next question.

She had us all laughing at her portrayal of Reverend Whitaker. He laughed the hardest of all. "I suppose I do get rather excited about the teaching of the Scriptures, do I not, girls?"

As Pocahontas gave him back his reading glasses and his Bible, she said, "No better teacher have I had, Reverend Whitaker. A man who loves his God should be the one who teaches about his God to

those who do not yet know him." I saw Reverend Whitaker look at her with a glimmer of hope.

It was late in the night before the gentlemen left and Reverend Whitaker retired to his bedchamber. I stayed in Pocahontas's room for a while, and we talked about Robert and John. We use their given names when we are alone. Pocahontas calls Master Rolfe "John," but I simply cannot. Master Rolfe is nearly ten years older than Pocahontas. That is old!

Pocahontas says that by the time some men are his age, they realize their limitations as well as their talents and are much easier to live with. She thinks Master Rolfe is as strong as Indian warriors she has known. We laughed as if we were two schoolgirls sharing secrets. Of course, we are!

Good night, Elizabeth. I wish you could meet Pocahontas. You would like her very much.

Your friend,

Abigail

Rock Hall

DECEMBER 18, 1613

Dear Elizabeth,

Such joy! Your family's generosity to us here again overwhelms me. Mrs. Sizemore was overjoyed with the quince preserves and the rose-petal potpourri you sent to her.

She also thanks you for the herbs. After my snakebite, Mrs. Sizemore has stored up every kind of medicinal herb she can find. Soon she is going to make the hospital planned for Mount Malady completely unnecessary. The sick can just come to Rock Hall.

Reverend Whitaker thanks your father for the most recently published *Book of Common Prayer*. He says it is such a thoughtful gift.

I was thrilled with my birthday gifts! The gold chain is perfect for keeping Mother's wedding ring safe. It is lovely and strong. The ring is all I have left of Mother. I will wear Mother's ring close to my heart all the days of my life. Please hug your papa for me.

Your dear mother's gift of sugar and spices thrilled me! Now I will have gingerbread this Christmas. I was so disappointed that Mrs. Sizemore used up our spices for the gingerbread she served when Pocahontas first arrived.

Never does a shipment come to me that your mother is not thinking of my most important needs. Again, she sends paper, ink, and seeds. Please thank her for the variety of seeds. I cannot wait until spring and planting season. My garden shall rival Mistress Pierce's garden yet!

Thank you! Thank you! Thank you! My only regret is that this ship will return to you with my letters and my presents for Christmas to your family much after Christmas has passed. Oh, one day would it not be wonderful if our letters could simply fly over the ocean to each other?

Your contented friend,

Abigail

Chipping Camden, England

DECEMBER 21, 1613

Dear Abigail,

I have slept little this last month. The orange and lemon trees arrived from Italy, but alas, the orangery was not ready. We tucked the trees in the buttery near the southern windows, and I pray they will not freeze and die.

The metalworkers brave the cold and have set up a smelting furnace on site. This time I am supervising every step of the process. According to my studies, I believe the leading was too weak the last time, so we have altered the formula for the grids. I am still not sure it will hold, but with additional height in the brick wall, brick columns at the corners, and the redesign of the metal grid for the mullioned windows, I am hopeful.

Christmas is almost here, but my aunt and uncle have excused me from having to entertain guests at the parties. They know I am single-minded and determined to get Uncle's citrus trees into the orangery as soon as possible. I miss my family at this time of year, and I think even more about you without your precious mother and father.

Your friend,

Elizabeth

Rock Hall

CHRISTMAS DAY, 1613

Dearest Elizabeth,

Merry Christmas! Soon the supply ship will bring you my gifts. Robert helped me make the special chess set for John. I have beautiful glass bead necklaces for you and your mother. I made them from beads made by the glassblowers in James Towne a few years ago. Tell John that Captain Smith used the beads to trade with the Indians. For your papa, I have a copy of the Lord's Prayer in my very best handwriting. There. Now he will know his urging of my lessons has not been in vain.

We will have a large gathering for Christmas dinner. Governor Gates, who will leave in a few months for England, Marshal Dale, Master Rolfe, Robert, and alas, many of the church ladies are all to arrive shortly for dinner. I have made gingerbread to share with them, thanks to your dear mother!

At church this morning, Reverend Whitaker spoke tenderly of the love of God who willingly sent his Son to earth in the form of a little baby—not a strong warrior—to win the world to himself through the power of his love for each of us. Pocahontas listened intently. If she decides to become a Christian, it will be of her own free will. Anyway, who could make Pocahontas do anything? She is very strong willed.

I must go now and help Mrs. Sizemore with the meal. It promises to be a feast. Please give my love to your father and mother and that dear brother of yours. Tell him I live with a real live Indian and we go to school together. That should impress his friends.

Your friend,

Abigail

Rock Hall

JANUARY 16, 1614

Dear Elizabeth,

We do not expect to see Master Rolfe or Robert here this week because the snowdrifts are several feet high. I milked the cows this morning and churned the butter. This is not a task I like to do, but Mrs. Sizemore has not been feeling well. I miss her directing my every move.

Today, I made her some pottage. She told me I will make a fine wife one day and then surprised me by asking about Master Sparkes. Mrs. Sizemore had a twinkle in her eye. "You are nearly eighteen. It is time to consider the attentions of the young man." Nearly eighteen? Why, that is ten months away! I am not ready to be courted, much less married!

"I like Master Sparkes," I told her. Hoping to discourage her questions, I added, "But he is so confident and impressed with himself."

"It takes a lot of courage to come to a new world, Abigail. Do not begrudge the young man his bold talk. He may just be bolstering up a fearsome spirit of his own."

It was a good thought from an unexpected source. I may talk with Mrs. Sizemore again about this.

Your friend,

Abigail

Rock Hall

JANUARY 20, 1614

Dear Elizabeth,

The ground is still covered with snow. Daily church services are suspended as it is now impossible to get across the river. Reverend Whitaker, always dutiful, rides Admiral to visit the families and the plantations.

Tonight he brought back word to us from Master Rolfe. His tobacco was somewhat well received in London, but the quality still does not rival the tobacco from the West Indies.

Pocahontas sniffed at that thought and said, "Wait until they taste the tobacco that has been curing since this fall. Then they will see that Master Rolfe's tobacco is the best in the world."

"Hmmm," said Reverend Whitaker. "I see you are a big fan of Master Rolfe."

Pocahontas quickly retorted, "Well, it was I who told him when to harvest this crop. I will take full credit if it is the world's finest tobacco yet."

More seriously, Reverend Whitaker is pleased with how well Pocahontas has learned the basics of our Christian faith. This past month, we worked on the Apostles' Creed. He takes each section of the creed and uses Bible verses to explain what the creed means.

Pocahontas told me her favorite part of the creed is about the Son who has redeemed her and all mankind. That, she says, is amazing. No more child sacrifices. No more fear of God. His Son—now her elder brother. This thought brings her much comfort as she ponders the ways of this English God and whether or not to put her trust in him.

I am so glad that the Lord has dealt with my bitter, angry heart. Pocahontas is a good friend. She and I are very different and yet very much the same. You would really like her, Elizabeth. I wish the two of you could meet.

Your friend,
Abigail

Chipping Camden, England

JANUARY 26, 1614

Dear Abigail,

Papa, Mother, and John arrived yesterday. As busy as I have been, the time has flown by. Yet, when I saw them, I realized just how much I have missed being with them.

Today we belatedly exchanged our Christmas gifts. Uncle gave everyone oranges from his new trees tucked happily away in the brand-new orangery. They smelled a bit of smoke from the fire we use on the coldest days to warm the orangery. I will have to work on that.

Mother gave me a ring that had belonged to her mother. John gave me one of his Latin books and a cipher book. Papa nodded and added his blessing to lessons from Master Sewell upon our return. I could not believe it!

Papa was eager to give me his gift, but said it must wait until this evening. He and Uncle exchanged glances all day. Then Papa blindfolded me and led me by the arm. I could tell by the smell of rich leather that we were in the library.

Papa removed my blindfold and, there at the window, I saw it. A six-times magnification telescope pointed at the heavens. "It is yours," said Papa. I could not believe my eyes.

Uncle nudged me over to the telescope, which was so much longer than the three-times one Uncle and I had shared. "Larger lenses need a longer time to refract the light," he explained.

I stood by the telescope and touched it gently. It had been so long since I had looked through one. I looked at Papa. "The package you took back to London?"

He replied, "Uncle agreed we should sell the three-times magnification telescope and purchase this new one. Go ahead," he said. "See if you can see Jupiter." I was astonished. Papa knew about Galileo's discovery several years ago using his six-times

magnification telescope! "And then I would very much like it, Elizabeth, if you would show me how to look through it."

I tried to look through the telescope, but the tears swimming in my eyes blurred the view. I used the sleeve of my dress to wipe the tears away. I blinked hard and then looked through the telescope again.

I gasped. The stars were so much clearer and more distinct than I had ever seen them before. Of course, that only started another flood of tears. I flung my arms around Papa and did not let go. All my disappointment and anger of the last few years melted away. I felt such tenderness for Papa as I had never known before.

Mother was crying. My aunt was crying. A tear ran down Uncle's face. Finally, the silence was broken by John who asked impatiently, "May I see the man in the moon now?"

Papa nodded, and I trained the telescope on the moon and showed John, to his great distress, that the "man in the moon" is but shadows and valleys on its surface.

Through my tears, I asked Papa to explain how all this had happened—especially his change of heart.

Papa said Uncle had made a bargain with him. "If Uncle removed his telescope and did not speak with you about it, and if you were willing to submit to the discipline of your elders, then Uncle wanted a chance to put a challenge in front of you."

"The orangery!" I said. *So Papa had known about it all along.*

"Yes, Uncle observed your precise drawings of the stars and your hand copies of the moon maps. He noticed your sense of perspective and order. When he became enchanted with an orangery he saw in Italy, he wanted to build one here. He decided it would be a wonderful opportunity for you to design a building to fit the needs of Italian citrus trees in the winters of England. He also knew, and I agreed, that the challenge would keep your mind off the stars—at least for a while."

"Did you really believe I could do it, Papa?" I asked.

"When I arrived here, your uncle showed me your orangery. The

winter sun glinted off the southern windows. I was speechless. And humbled. I have underestimated the gifts the good Lord has given you."

"In addition to stitchery?" I asked, teasing.

"I have been stubborn, I know, but I wanted you to know all you needed for the calling you have before you of wife and mother. Yet now I realize that perhaps you will design the home in which you will be a wife and mother! I will provide you with a tutor for whatever—in good reason—you desire to learn." Papa beamed with pride.

I whispered, "Thank you, Papa. Thank you for teaching me to read and write and opening up this world to me. I am forever grateful."

It is four o'clock in the morning, and I cannot go to sleep. My life today has been changed forever and ever. It is still not possible as a girl to go to Oxford or Cambridge, but Papa will help me learn. Abigail, Papa—*my* Papa—wants me to learn!

With a grateful heart,

Elizabeth

Rock Hall

FEBRUARY 6, 1614

Dear Elizabeth,

Governor Gates returns soon to England on the *Elizabeth*. He is determined to wrap up this Pocahontas problem before he goes. He is very angry that Chief Powhatan will not bargain for his daughter. The pawn in their political game is becoming worthless to them. It has been nearly a year, and yet Pocahontas remains a hostage here with not a word from her father. It makes me fearful for her. What will they do with her?

I overheard Reverend Whitaker and Master Rolfe speak quietly. They, too, are worried. Oh, Elizabeth, what is to become of Pocahontas?

Your worried friend,

Abigail

Rock Hall

FEBRUARY 15, 1614

Dear Elizabeth,

Tonight, Master Rolfe and Reverend Whitaker met and spoke in low, hushed voices for several hours. Master Rolfe seemed very agitated. He paced the floor. He knelt and prayed with Reverend Whitaker.

Something is about to happen. I can feel it. I am frightened, especially for Pocahontas. She was away with the church ladies tonight for more etiquette lessons in the ways of English royalty. After all, she is a princess.

I strained to overhear what Master Rolfe was saying, but I only caught bits and pieces of the conversation. Reverend Whitaker encouraged Master Rolfe to search his heart and see if his desires were pure. Master Rolfe said that he does not want anything he desires to be outside of God's will and plan for himself or the colony.

I did overhear them both pray that Pocahontas would come to an understanding of God's mercy and grace. Master Rolfe seems extremely troubled in his spirit. Reverend Whitaker is a wise and good counselor, though, and should be able to help him.

All I know is that things are about to change. I can sense it in all the activity. The church ladies have stepped up their English princess lessons for Pocahontas. Reverend Whitaker has increased his lessons in the Scriptures. He told me that he wants Pocahontas to understand as much of the Bible as possible without delay.

Without delay? What is the hurry? Could it be that soon Pocahontas will be leaving us? Is this why Master Rolfe is so upset?

Your troubled friend,

Abigail

Rock Hall

February 17, 1614

Dear Elizabeth,

Master Rolfe came over tonight. Again, he and Reverend Whitaker went to the library to speak quietly. Mrs. Sizemore and Pocahontas are with the other church ladies—more lessons.

Reverend Whitaker asked me to serve them a hot drink. I was happy to do it because I wanted to find out what is going on. I brought in the leather jugs of steaming cider. I added some of the sweets that your mother sent for this very important conversation.

When I took the tray to the library, Reverend Whitaker was reading a very long letter. I recognized the handwriting as Master Rolfe's. When I served Reverend Whitaker, I saw that the letter was addressed to Marshal Dale. What could it say?

Master Rolfe looked deeply troubled. He sat on the edge of his chair and anxiously waited for Reverend Whitaker's response. I lingered as long as I dared. "Might I serve you anything else?" I asked Master Rolfe. "Is your cider hot enough? Is there anything you need?"

I think Reverend Whitaker caught on, because he removed his spectacles and said coolly, "Thank you, Abigail. We appreciate your hospitality, but we are fine."

What is so important that Master Rolfe had to put it in writing? Could he not simply speak to Marshal Dale himself? What could Master Rolfe have written that needed Reverend Whitaker's review? Why all the secrecy?

I just know it has to do with Pocahontas, but what?

Your friend,

Abigail

Rock Hall

February 18, 1614

Dear Elizabeth,

Now I am sure something is about to happen. Governor Gates, Marshal Dale, Master Hamor, and Master Rolfe all came to Rock Hall today to meet with Reverend Whitaker. Several times I overheard the name Chief Powhatan.

Pocahontas has been with us so long now that I no longer think of her as a hostage but as my friend. I forget that, to the leaders, she is just a political pawn to use in the struggle to establish a colony for England. I fear greatly for her.

I prepared the noonday meal for the gentlemen. I am afraid I rushed, and it was not my best cooking. I did not want to miss an opportunity to hear what they were discussing. I lingered over my service, as quiet as a church mouse so they would forget I was there.

Governor Gates leaves in a few days for England and Marshal Dale will be the deputy governor in his stead. I heard Master Rolfe whisper to Master Hamor that Deputy Governor Dale likely will force Chief Powhatan's hand and use Pocahontas to do so. Was it true? I took my time serving, desperately wanting to hear every word of this conversation.

I was fairly certain the men had taken no notice of me, but then Reverend Whitaker looked up. He came close to me with the pretense of asking that I serve more root vegetables. Then he leaned forward and whispered sternly in my ear, "Not a word of this to Pocahontas."

I continued about my serving duties as quietly as possible. Then I heard Master Rolfe ask Deputy Governor Dale, "What, sir, do you think should be done with the princess Pocahontas?"

Deputy Governor Dale replied, "I would not like to see her returned to her people just yet. She has not yet made a commitment to Christ. It is my earnest hope and prayer that she would know the living God and receive him as her own. Nonetheless ...”

“Yes?” Master Rolfe prompted, leaning forward.

“Nonetheless, we must do what is for the good of the colony and England. Rest assured, we will take all possible measures to make peace with Chief Powhatan through negotiation and bargaining. But we will do battle, if we must. It will soon be spring,” he continued, “and our soldiers have been drilling and training all winter long. They will be fit for battle, if need be.”

“But ... what about Pocahontas then?”

Reverend Whitaker said, “Even if Pocahontas leaves us soon, she has had much teaching in the catechism and the Scriptures. She is an intelligent girl, and I am sure that the Word of God has penetrated her heart, if not her will as yet.” He looked steadily at Deputy Governor Dale and Governor Gates. “But know this, gentlemen. I will not perform any rite of baptism without the full assurance of her commitment of heart, soul, mind, and strength to the Lord Jesus Christ. As much as my heart hungers for her to be fully assured of the truth of Jesus Christ, of his love and saving grace toward her, I will never perform the sacred rite of baptism for political ends.”

I was proud of Reverend Whitaker for refusing to hurry Pocahontas’s training in the ways of Christianity so he could baptize her. He was not going to let these men use Pocahontas in some political game. They would not be bragging about their Indian convert when in London, all puffed up about sending their convert back to her heathen people to Christianize them.

Reverend Whitaker gazed steadily at the two men across from him until finally Governor Gates said, “Why of course, Alexander, we yield to you on matters of religion. Pocahontas will not be baptized until you are assured that she has renounced her gods and accepted the one true God.”

The way he said it gave me chills. I could see that the saving of Pocahontas’s soul was secondary to the political needs at hand.

I also saw how Master Rolfe shot a pleading look at Reverend Whitaker.

Master Rolfe is in great torment. He is a valiant colonist, through and through, and he has always been obedient to the authorities over him. Yet, now, I can see in his eyes that he is greatly disturbed. I do think he dearly loves my friend Pocahontas. No wonder he and Reverend Whitaker have had so many meetings lately. They are both concerned about the increased talk of using Pocahontas as a ransom for peace or as a challenge for war with the Indians.

I must end now. My candle is getting very low. I will write again soon. Please pray that Pocahontas will be protected.

Fearfully,

Abigail

Rock Hall

February 23, 1614

Dear Elizabeth,

Master Rolfe and Robert visited today. Mrs. Sizemore and Reverend Whitaker withdrew and gave us time together, something they have rarely done before. Do they know the time is short?

Pocahontas is no fool. As soon as we were alone, she faced Master Rolfe and asked, "John, a decision has been made about me, am I right?"

Master Rolfe and Robert looked at each other. I was surprised, for I had never before heard Pocahontas call Master Rolfe by his given name. He took Pocahontas by the hand, led her to a chair, and bade her sit down.

He then knelt by her chair, looked in her eyes, and said, "I will not keep anything from you, Pocahontas. The leaders are discussing what should be done about your father, Chief Powhatan, and the hostilities between our two peoples. The leaders are frustrated because so much time has passed, and your father has not negotiated for your release. In fact, your father has not even inquired about your well-being."

I saw the look in Pocahontas's eyes as she fought back tears. I tried to imagine how she must feel. Her father has abandoned her. She has begun to find true love with John. She has found friends in Reverend Whitaker, Mrs. Sizemore, and me. She has begun to get used to English ways, and has learned to speak and even read English. She has even begun to know our God.

Now, all this could be stripped from her, just like the English stripped her Indian life from her last April when she was captured by Captain Argall. I cannot even imagine the pain and confusion she must be feeling.

Master Rolfe continued, "Pocahontas, there is talk about trying to force your father's hand concerning you."

Pocahontas replied, "He will never deal with the English. Not even for me—his own daughter, his Matoaka." Pocahontas turned her face away from Master Rolfe, then continued, "Ever since I was a young girl and knew Captain Smith, I found the English a challenging sort. Stupid at times, but not evil. I felt we could find a way to live together. The English have killed so many of my people, and my people have killed so many of the English." Pocahontas stopped when she said this and looked at me. "There has been great pain and many sacrifices on both sides." Then Pocahontas stood up and began to pace the room. "No more!" she said. "John, this must stop!"

Master Rolfe asked, "But Pocahontas, what can we do?"

"I do not know, but there must be a way for both the English and my people to live together in peace."

Robert stepped forward and said, "John, it is likely the leaders will send an emissary to Chief Powhatan to present the arrangement that Deputy Governor Dale decides upon. Let us volunteer. If anyone can speak to the ability of the English to get along with the Indians, it is you. And I will accompany you."

Pocahontas brightened. "Yes, John, you can tell my father about me. He may listen to you. You could explain about my good treatment at the hands of the English and my heart's desire that we all find a path to peace."

I said, "That is too dangerous! Master Rolfe and Robert might be killed if the Indians think the English are there to trick or hurt them. After all, it was the English who tricked you into coming onto the *Treasurer* and then abducted you." I blushed when I realized I had called Master Sparkes by his given name, but I do not think he noticed.

Master Rolfe quickly answered, "I will take that risk."

Robert added, "I, as well."

Pocahontas smiled broadly. "Then it is settled."

Master Rolfe and Robert decided to speak with Reverend Whitaker and seek his counsel concerning the idea. Pocahontas and

I sat on the steps outside the library, but we could hear very little. Finally, after what seemed an eternity, they opened the door.

Reverend Whitaker laughed as he saw the two of us huddled together on the steps. "My, my, girls, what have we here? Should we fill you in or have you heard every word already?"

We rushed into the library and said, "Do, please, tell us!"

Reverend Whitaker explained that he thought the plan was sound and that it might lead to peace at last. Pocahontas sighed with relief and asked if he thought Deputy Governor Dale would approve. Reverend Whitaker then explained the plan in detail. It was settled. In a fortnight, Deputy Governor Dale and at least 150 men would sail up to Matchcot, where Chief Powhatan currently resides. They would seek to seal an agreement for the return of Pocahontas or begin the war with the tribes.

Pocahontas exclaimed, "Oh, no! Not war!"

Reverend Whitaker said, "You must take courage, dear Pocahontas. God loves you and your people very much. He knows what is in your heart. He knows your desire for peace with the English and an end to all the killing. He will not forsake you. Take heart."

I watched Pocahontas's face. She seemed deeply affected in a way I had not seen as she pondered Reverend Whitaker's words.

"Master Rolfe, Master Sparkes, and I will travel to Deputy Governor Dale's home to discuss this plan with him. Pray, girls. Pray that he sees the wisdom in sending Master Rolfe to speak with Chief Powhatan. Pray for peace."

When the men left, Pocahontas and I stood with our arms around each other and waved to them. Mrs. Sizemore came in with two mugs of steaming cider and gave us both a hug.

I suppose she knows more than we thought she did. No wonder the church ladies have been stepping up the pace of Pocahontas's English lady lessons.

As we got ready for bed, Pocahontas asked me, "Do you think I can do as Reverend Whitaker asked? May I pray to the English

God? I have not yet decided, Abigail, if I will renounce Ahone and Okee. Will your God hear me?"

"Of course. He wants you to pray to him. He wants you to know his heart toward you, dear friend. Would you like to pray with me?"

Then, as we knelt down by the bed in my room, I had the privilege of hearing a pure heart poured out before a loving God. I sense that Pocahontas is ready to receive the gift of salvation from our heavenly Father. She will make her decision in time.

Your exhausted but encouraged friend,

Abigail

Rock Hall

FEBRUARY 26, 1614

Dear Elizabeth,

It is settled. Reverend Whitaker told us at our noonday meal that Deputy Governor Dale has agreed. Master Rolfe and Robert will be the emissaries to Chief Powhatan.

The soldiers across the river at Henricus drill daily. Here at Coxendale, other men are drilling as well. It is strange to hear the sounds of war when peace is what is on our hearts.

Robert said Deputy Governor Dale is determined to win—one way or the other. It causes me grave concern. Will Robert and Master Rolfe be caught up in the battle? Will they return to us? Will Chief Powhatan negotiate with them or give the order for them to be killed?

I cannot bear the thought of arrows piercing these brave men. That is why I shall give no thought to a courtship with Robert. I will not lose another person I care about to an Indian arrow.

Your friend,

Abigail

London, England

FEBRUARY 28, 1614

My Dear Abigail,

Your letters and wonderful Christmas gifts just reached us. John marvels at the chess set, and I marvel that your Master Sparkes could carve such a beautiful gift. You must write to me more about him. I cannot help noticing that your letters speak of him more often and with greater tenderness.

I stayed up until the early hours of the morning to read your letters. You are a true adventurer. I am neither brave nor adventurous. Do you know that Temperance, despite all the horrible tales she tells me, sometimes thinks of returning to Virginia? She has begun to correspond with a young captain there, George Yeardley. Is it to Virginia or to Captain Yeardley that she wishes to return?

Your letters let me know that you and Pocahontas are friends. I am glad. I have been praying for you to find someone there in Virginia who can share your life.

Your friend,

Elizabeth

P.S. Papa said to tell you he keeps your elegant writing of the Lord's Prayer on his desk. He says you will make a fine English woman yet. Ha! If he only knew what I know—climbing trees, racing horses, muddy hands, snakebites, and a great disdain for English recipes (all except for gingerbread, of course)!

Rock Hall

March 1, 1614

Dear Elizabeth,

This past week, Pocahontas asked me to read to her often from the Bible. I heard her muffled prayers in the quiet of her room. She has refused visits from Master Rolfe and has kept much to herself.

Today, she asked Reverend Whitaker if she might speak with him in private. They spent much of the day in the library with the door shut. When they finally came out, Reverend Whitaker had a twinkle in his eye. Of course, I peppered him with questions about what they talked about, but he said simply, "Abigail, you know that some things are kept private."

I asked Pocahontas what she and the Reverend spoke about, and she simply said, "Important matters."

It is not like Pocahontas to be this secretive. Of course, I am dying to know what is going on, but I must respect my friend and be patient. Not exactly my best quality.

Your friend,

Abigail

Rock Hall

MARCH 3, 1614

Dear Elizabeth,

Today Pocahontas asked Reverend Whitaker if she and I could go for a ride on Admiral. Reverend Whitaker had planned to visit the nearby settlement at Bermuda Nether Hundred and counsel with the parishioners there, but he changed his plans to accommodate Pocahontas's request.

Mrs. Sizemore packed us a noonday meal in a basket while Pocahontas saddled Admiral. I hovered around Reverend Whitaker with the hope he would say something—anything—about how Pocahontas was acting. He said nothing.

Pocahontas trotted up from the barn and gave me a hand up onto Admiral's back. We rode a long time and said nothing—both enjoying our freedom. It was an unseasonably warm day, and Admiral seemed to enjoy the unrestrained ride as well.

We had strict instructions from Reverend Whitaker not to go too far. Somehow, Pocahontas had taken Admiral on a circuitous route, which made it feel like we had been riding forever, even though we were really near where we had started. We dismounted near the bank of the James River some distance from the parsonage but still within view of the forts.

We spread our meal on a blanket by the river and spoke of many things. She asked about my mother and father and what life was like in England before I came to Virginia. She asked about you and Temperance and my other friends in England. She told me about her brothers and sisters and her mother. She spoke of her father and said she had been hurt deeply by his lack of interest in her rescue.

Then Pocahontas shared with me about her year at Rock Hall. She said, "You really did not like me when I first arrived!"

"Did it show that much?" I asked. We both laughed, for we knew

that I had been horrible to her. I had let her know in every way possible that I could not stand to be near her.

"Abigail, you were true. I have always known where I stand with you. You do not treat me as a political pawn. You do not treat me as a project—an Indian to be converted or dressed up to become an English princess. You have always, *always* been absolutely honest with me about what you think." Pocahontas paused for a moment, and then added, "It hurt at times."

"I am sorry for that. I had so much anger and pain in my heart about my mother and father. I took it out on you."

"I know that now."

"Pocahontas, I never in a million years thought you and I would be friends." Again we laughed for we both knew our friendship was an unlikely miracle. I hugged her and added, "Now we are friends forever, no matter what happens."

Then Pocahontas asked me if I still hated her father. I was caught up short. My heart felt pierced.

"Your father? Why do you ask?"

"It was my father who ordered the attack that killed your father. It was my father who ordered the Powhatans to cease trading with the English, which caused your mother to starve to death."

My heart lurched inside me and told me the answer. I knew I must be honest with Pocahontas.

"I have not thought about this for a long time. When the Lord began to work on my heart about my feelings toward you, I knew I was taking my pain and anger toward your father and placing it on you. After all, you are the princess Pocahontas, the daughter of the great Indian chief who destroyed my family. Somehow, though, over time, I was able to separate my feelings for you from my feelings for your father."

"You began to see me as someone different?"

"Yes. Even though I knew in the back of my mind that you are Chief Powhatan's cherished daughter, as they all said in James Towne. I began to see that you were not at all like him. You brought corn to the English for several years. You befriended Captain Smith. You saved Henry Spelman's life. I guess I did eventually see you as different from him."

"If I am returned to my father, I will again be Princess Pocahontas, Princess of the Powhatans and a servant to my father. I must do his will."

"Must you? There is a higher calling on your life now, Pocahontas. Perhaps the reason you were taken from your people and placed with us for this year is so you could tell the truth about the English—that we are not all so bad—and that there is a God who loves them so much that he became the final sacrifice for them."

"But if I become my father's daughter again, will your hatred for him become hatred for me?"

We remained very quiet. Both of us had asked the other very difficult questions. They were true and strong questions deserving of true and strong answers. We rode silently back to Rock Hall. Admiral seemed to sense our deep thoughts as he plodded slowly back. Both Pocahontas and I know that the agreement for her return will take place very soon. Our time together at Rock Hall is short. Pocahontas and I may be friends for life, but without these questions settled, we will always wonder how true our friendship really was.

As I prayed tonight, I realized that Pocahontas's question has seared my heart. The Lord has shown me in my heart's response that I do harbor hatred toward the father of the friend my Lord has given me. What will I do with that hatred?

It is a troubling, but necessary, question.

Your friend,

Abigail

Rock Hall

MARCH 6, 1614

Dear Elizabeth,

Yesterday I worked alone in my garden. It is there, close to the earth, that I feel closest to God. I took my hoe and turned the soil over and over to prepare it for spring planting. But it was the soil of my heart that was really being plowed by the Spirit of God. The Lord was dealing with me as I worked. Pocahontas's question ran through my mind again and again, but I knew the question behind the question.

Pocahontas knew I had forgiven *her*. She knew I had worked it all out in my mind. I had mixed up my hatred of her with my hatred of her father and his control over my family's fate. She knew that the ultimate question I had to answer was whether I could forgive her father.

Forgive the man who caused my parents' deaths? Forgive the man who had the power to spare me all this heartache and pain, but did not? Forgive the man who has no regrets about what he has done? Just forgive him?

These questions swirled around in my mind. What difference does it make anyway? I am not going to meet him—we could even be at war with him in just a few short weeks. What does it matter?

I tugged and tugged at some weeds that had deeper roots than usual. I pressed down hard on my hoe with my foot to try to lift up the roots, but I could not get them to budge. I fell to the ground exhausted.

With dirt covering my face and hands, I began to sob uncontrollably. All the years of pain and loneliness came crashing in on me. I have tried to be so brave. I have tried to be thankful for the goodness of God. After all, the Pierces, Reverend Whitaker, and Mrs. Sizemore have all taken very good care of me. And I do appreciate them. Really I do.

It is just that there is a terrible ache inside. I can no longer feel the arms of a mother around me or the strong hand of a father on my shoulder. I can no longer remember the sound of their voices.

When I think of all I have lost, a terrible, horrible, agonizing ache presses on my heart.

Did I hate Chief Powhatan? Yes! *Yes*! I hated him with all my heart. If only he had shown compassion—or even just left us alone—Mother and Father would be alive today.

I pounded the ground with my fist and hurled question after question at God. Why had he allowed this to happen? Could not he have stopped Chief Powhatan? Could not he have taken only my father or my mother—why did he let both of them die?

I lay in the garden, covered in dirt and mud, finally spent and silent. My face was wet with tears, my heart heavy, and my soul distraught. I was finished with my questions.

I was so quiet that I should have heard Reverend Whitaker enter through the garden gate. He sat down beside me and pulled a worn Bible from his jacket.

"Abigail," he said very softly, "you are asking important questions. Questions of the heart. Questions of life. There is not a generation that passes that does not face and ask these same questions. Is God really there for you? Is he there for you when all of life's circumstances seem to shout otherwise? Can you trust him? With your mother? Your father? With your own life?"

"I do not know," I admitted. "I read my Bible faithfully, but I do not know."

"You know much *about* him, Abigail, but do you know him? Can you abandon yourself to him and know he loves you? Can you, in adversity as well as joy, in blessings as well as difficulties, trust your heavenly Father?"

I wrapped my arms around my knees and pulled them up close to my chest. "If I forgive Chief Powhatan, then what do I have left?"

"Ah," answered Reverend Whitaker. "We get to the heart of it finally." Reverend Whitaker was silent for several minutes and then

said, "Are you afraid that if you let go of your anger and hatred of Chief Powhatan that somehow you will disgrace the memory of your own father?"

I began to cry again, but this time the tears were soothing and cleansing. The questions Reverend Whitaker was putting to me now were those that had whirled around in my heart these last four years.

I had been afraid to face them. Somehow, hearing him ask them out loud made them less frightening. Yes, it was true. Somehow my hatred of Chief Powhatan keeps the memory of my parents alive. It is as if that is the only way I know to protect them or at least protect their memories.

"Jesus knew we needed God's help to forgive those who hurt us. It is not something you can do on your own. He will help you forgive. Here," he said, handing me his Bible, "let God speak to you."

He gave me a hug and walked quietly away. I sat for a few minutes with the tears still sliding down my face. Before I even opened the Bible, I knelt there in my garden and forgave Chief Powhatan and even God for taking away my parents. The numbness in my heart began to seep away as I opened the Bible to Psalm 40 and read:

> *I waited patiently for the LORD;*
> *He turned to me and heard my cry.*
> *He lifted me out of the slimy pit, Out of the mud and mire;*
> *He set my feet on a rock*
> *And gave me a firm place to stand.*
> *He put a new song in my mouth, a hymn of praise to our God.*
> *Many will see and fear and put their trust in the LORD.*

Suddenly, I knew what I must do. I jumped up and brushed myself off. I tucked Reverend Whitaker's Bible under my arm and ran back to the parsonage. I found Pocahontas in the barn, grooming Admiral. I am sure I looked frightful with my dirty face showing streaks where the tears had been. "Pocahontas, you were right. I did hate your father. I hated him with all my being—but no more. I did not even realize how much hatred I carried in my heart until the Lord showed me why I could not let it go."

"What did he show you?" she asked.

"It was sin—pure sin—and it was keeping me from trusting him with my life as an orphan. I am so sorry I could not see it before. It must have caused you great pain. Dear friend, will you forgive me for hurting you by carrying so much hatred in my heart toward your father?"

"Forgive you? I do not understand."

"My hatred and anger have been festering inside me for four years. When you came, I did not want to be around you. As I got to know you, I let my anger toward you slip away. But I kept my anger and hatred toward your father. When I confessed this to God in the garden, I asked him to take away my hatred."

"And did he?" she asked.

"Well, he surprised me. He told me to lay it down. It was I who took up this hatred, and I was the one who would have to lay it down again. Then he told me to trust him to fill up the holes in my heart. I do, now. I really do. It may take time, and I may struggle with it daily for some time, but I know now that he will do it. A new song has come in my heart, one I have not heard for a very long time. Yet, Pocahontas, I see now how much my sin must have hurt you all this time we have been living here at Rock Hall together."

"Yes, it has hurt me. I will not lie to you."

"You are lonely too. You also miss your father and your whole family. I would never let you speak of him. I said horrible things about him. I tried to feed your own sadness about how he would not negotiate for you. I wanted you to hurt because of your father as much as I hurt because of him."

The Indian girl stood still as a statue, waiting.

"Princess Pocahontas," I said, "daughter of the king of great and mighty tribes, will you forgive me for such horrible, cruel behavior?"

183

Pocahontas touched Admiral with tears in her eyes. "Yes," she answered.

We threw our arms around each other. I have never been so full of joy. We walked back to the parsonage arm in arm, happy and content in the knowledge that our friendship was forever.

Your friend,

Abigail

Rock Hall

MARCH 18, 1614

Dear Elizabeth,

Today Master Rolfe and Robert came to visit. In a few days, they will leave with Deputy Governor Dale and some 150 men to sail to Matchcot, home of Chief Powhatan, to meet with him.

Master Rolfe spent more than an hour alone with Reverend Whitaker. Robert explained to me that John is very much in love with the princess Pocahontas but dares not express it to Deputy Governor Dale. He has struggled with his feelings for months and has frequently sought the counsel of Reverend Whitaker, because he knows the Bible would not have him marry someone who does not share his faith in Christ. He had hoped that Pocahontas would become a Christian, but if she will not, he cannot marry her.

It has been an agonizing but necessary decision. It must be particularly difficult for him to say good-bye to Pocahontas now. He has never expressed his feelings to her. He has remained a faithful friend.

Robert told me that, at one point, Master Rolfe spent days writing out his thoughts about the princess in a letter to Deputy Governor Dale. In the letter, he asked for approval to marry Pocahontas, but he withheld the letter because Pocahontas had not yet decided to become a Christian. Without that decision first, she could never be his wife.

I asked Robert where the letter was now. He told me that he thought Reverend Whitaker was keeping it safe. Robert said that John's love for Pocahontas is very strong and deep, but deeper still is his commitment and love for the Lord. His hopes that she would come to know and receive the Lord Jesus were dashed when all this talk of returning her to Chief Powhatan began. Robert said that Reverend Whitaker was especially moved by Master Rolfe's commitment to Pocahontas. They both agreed that neither would

push the question of her salvation because of their own desires to see her become a Christian.

Pocahontas and Master Rolfe took a long walk together, while I showed Robert some of my new plants in the garden. When they returned, Reverend Whitaker gathered us in the library with Master Hamor, who had just arrived. Master Hamor told Master Rolfe and Robert that the plans for the journey are now finalized.

Master Hamor explained that Deputy Governor Dale had several ships ready for the journey, and that Master Rolfe and Robert needed to leave now to discuss how to negotiate for Pocahontas's ransom. Pocahontas will be returned to Chief Powhatan if he returns all English weapons and all other prisoners, and if he provides a ship full of corn. If the negotiations fail, then Deputy Governor Dale is prepared to begin the battle right then and there.

Pocahontas asked, "How will 150 English fare against a thousand of my father's best warriors?" Pocahontas and I looked at each other. We were both afraid for Master Rolfe and Robert.

"The soldiers will be heavily armed and protected by armor," Master Hamor said. "Princess Pocahontas, you are to come with us on the ship." We all looked at each other with stunned expressions. "Deputy Governor Dale suspects that your father will not deal unless he knows you are well treated. He asked me to tell you to ready yourself."

Reverend Whitaker must have read my mind. "Might I recommend that Miss Matthews accompany the princess? She can tend to her needs."

Master Hamor thought for a moment. "It might help the negotiations with the chief if he knows the English have honored his daughter as the princess she is. Hmmmm ... a handmaid might be a good addition to the plan. I will check with Deputy Governor Dale."

After he left, Master Rolfe, Robert, Pocahontas, Reverend Whitaker, and I sat in the library and tried to sip cider and make

conversation. Master Hamor said we should expect to sail in three days. I swallowed hard.

Three days until I am face-to-face with these Indians. Will they harm us? Will they try to take Pocahontas without paying the ransom? Will a battle break out where they kill us too? I shivered at the thought of arrows piercing our bodies.

"Reverend Whitaker, I must thank you for your quick thinking to ask about Abigail," said Pocahontas. "She has been a constant companion this last year and a good friend."

No one wanted to talk about the obvious—that none of us may be with Pocahontas again after this week. Then Master Rolfe and Robert left. After Pocahontas went up to bed, it was just Reverend Whitaker and me sipping our cider.

"John Rolfe loves Pocahontas," I said boldly.

"Yes, I know," he replied.

"Well, what are you going to do about it?"

"What should I do? It is out of my hands."

"No, it is not. You have in your safekeeping a letter that could change everything."

Reverend Whitaker was startled. "How do you know about the letter?"

"Robert. Master Rolfe must have told him." We were silent for a while and then I said, "Well, I just thought you should know that I know."

Elizabeth, there is not much time now. In a few days, we leave on the *Treasurer.* I fear for our lives.

Your friend,

Abigail

Rock Hall

MARCH 21, 1614

Dear Elizabeth,

We have not seen Master Rolfe or Robert for the last few days. They are meeting daily with Deputy Governor Dale.

Reverend Whitaker prayed for us tonight. Then just as I was leaving to go to my room, he called me back to the library. He gave me a small leather folio and told me to open it. I did. Inside was a letter several pages long. I saw this was the letter Master Rolfe had given to Reverend Whitaker.

"Abigail Matthews, this is now entrusted to your care."

"But what shall I do with it?"

He said, "The Lord will show you at the proper time."

I did not understand what he meant, but I hugged him and hurried to my room to place the leather folio with my belongings.

Your friend,

Abigail

The Treasurer

MARCH 22, 1614

Dear Elizabeth,

How odd to be on this ship, the *Treasurer*. How much stranger still for Pocahontas. She has not been on this ship since Japazaws sold her to the English for a copper kettle. We are staying in the gunner's cabin, the very room that Pocahontas was locked in when she was abducted. There is no lock on the door now.

Pocahontas is quiet and reads her Bible. She has asked me several times to read the more difficult passages to her. She spends much time in what appears to me to be prayer. Whether she is praying to Ahone or God, I do not know.

Deputy Governor Dale wants Chief Powhatan to know he means business. He has told the Indians he can come in peace or war, but the choice is that of Chief Powhatan.

Your friend,

Abigail

The Treasurer

MARCH 24, 1614

Dear Elizabeth,

What a horrible day! When Deputy Governor Dale again spread the word to the Indians that he comes for peace or war, he got an answer. Showers of arrows came from everywhere and wounded one of our men.

That was all it took. The men went ashore. They burned some 40 houses, took food and other goods, and killed five or six Indians. Deputy Governor Dale knows the message will soon get to Chief Powhatan that he means business. The chief must deal regarding Pocahontas or war will begin.

Pocahontas is in great distress and remains secluded in the gunner's cabin of the *Treasurer*. I am to be with her at all times. I can tell she is in much agony. I try to be very quiet. Sometimes the best thing a friend can do is just be there.

Your friend,

Abigail

The Treasurer

MARCH 26, 1614

Dear Elizabeth,

We have been anchored here at Matchcot, where Chief Powhatan is supposed to be, for two days. But nothing has happened. No Indians. No arrows. No sounds.

Then, suddenly, hundreds and hundreds of Indians with bows and arrows stood on the shore. Our men also went ashore, protected in armor and well armed. Would anyone fire the first shot? The Indians made no show of fear. They walked up and down and demanded to know where our king was. They wanted to speak to him.

Deputy Governor Dale said that if the Indians attacked, they were ready for war, but he asked if they could send a message to Chief Powhatan. Deputy Governor Dale has given them until noon tomorrow. Then the fight will begin. He even promised to give them a warning by trumpet and drum before the attack.

While we were waiting, two of Pocahontas' brothers arrived. They wanted to meet with their sister for proof that she was all right. They carried no weapons.

Master Rolfe and Robert came to the gunner's cabin to get Pocahontas. I watched as she walked on the riverbank with her guards to meet them. Her brothers seemed overjoyed to see her. I could not understand what they were saying, but I could tell they thought she looked well. They talked for a long time.

Pocahontas explained to Deputy Governor Dale that her brothers would send word to her father that she is well, that she should be redeemed by the chief, and that a peace should be concluded between the two peoples. In exchange for the two brothers coming on board to stay, Master Rolfe and Robert would be dispatched to Chief Powhatan to conduct the negotiation.

Master Rolfe looked back at Pocahontas, who nodded ever so slightly at him. The look in their eyes spoke volumes, however, and

I thought of the letter waiting in the pocket of my jacket in the gunner's cabin.

Robert tipped his helmet to me and seemed much more self-assured than I felt, but then I remembered what Mrs. Sizemore had said. I waved to him. Pocahontas and I stared as the two men walked with the Indians into the forest along the shoreline.

For most of the afternoon, Pocahontas and her brothers visited with each other on the ship. They spoke in their native language, so I could not understand what was said. I could tell that they were glad to be together again. Later that afternoon, Pocahontas's brothers were given food. Pocahontas came to find me.

"Abigail, I must tell you some things that you can later share with John—especially if tomorrow I am redeemed by my father. I could not say anything until now."

"This sounds important."

"Yes, it is. Not long ago, I decided to forsake Ahone and Okee and receive Jesus Christ as my Lord and Savior. I now worship the English God. I asked Reverend Whitaker not to say anything to you or anyone for a long while."

"But why?" I asked, joy filling my heart.

"I needed to know if this choice I had made would be strong. I needed to know if I would be faithful to God no matter what happened. When I first heard of the plan to attempt peace by negotiating for my return, I struggled with my own desires. I wanted to stay at Rock Hall with you and Reverend Whitaker. And I wanted to stay with John. Yet, I also thought a great deal about what you had said to me concerning a higher calling. I thought of all that God did to sacrifice his own Son's life for me, and I found that I wanted to serve him more than anything—even if it meant I would lose my friends and my new life."

"Do you believe you *will* lose your life with us?" I asked.

"I do not know. Perhaps it is in returning to my people that peace will finally be made between our two peoples. Perhaps I will

be able to tell them about the God who does not require human sacrifice."

I grabbed her hand then. Words failed me. Pocahontas' voice was so soft I had to lean close to hear.

"I do not know what will happen tomorrow when John and Robert return, but I know this. I know that God loves me and he loves you. I know he will keep our two hearts bound together in friendship forever. Thank you for showing me the breadth and depth of the forgiveness of God. When you were able to forgive my father, I knew then that your God is able to do wondrous things. I knew then he could even make peace between our two peoples. What I did not know was that this might require me to return to my people. Yet I am willing if that is what God wants for me."

"Oh, Pocahontas, I do not want you to go. You are more than my friend. You are like a sister to me. There must be another way."

"The Lord will watch between me and you, Abigail. He will do what is right."

"Pocahontas, do you know of Master Rolfe's deep love for you?"

"I have suspected it for some time, but I knew he was troubled."

"The Scriptures speak of not being married to an unbeliever. He would never have wanted you to know of his love before you had made your own decision about whether or not to believe in Jesus. He spoke with Reverend Whitaker, though."

"John is a good man. Robert too, Abigail."

"I will miss our talks, Pocahontas."

"Perhaps if there is peace, we can visit again."

We hugged each other, and Pocahontas returned to her brothers. I stayed in the cabin a long time and prayed. Suddenly, I knew what God wanted me to do. I grabbed the leather folio and sought out Master Hamor.

"Master Hamor, sir, may I have a word with you?"

"Certainly, Miss Matthews, what might I do for you?

"Reverend Whitaker entrusted a special letter to me, and now I will entrust it to you."

He looked at me quizzically, but took the leather folio. He found a quiet spot on the ship, sat down, and opened the folio. I had not read the letter, but I could guess what it said. I watched him read it once. Then twice. Then once more. He slowly folded the letter and put it back in the leather folio. Then he put the folio in his jacket pocket and turned to watch the river.

After what seemed like hours, I saw him stride over to Deputy Governor Dale. The two of them went below to the Captain's quarters.

That night Pocahontas and I prayed together. We prayed for safety for Master Rolfe and Robert. We prayed for God's will. We prayed for peace. We thanked God for each other. I did not say anything about the letter—after all, I really did not know what was in it.

I do not think either Pocahontas or I slept well that night.

Your friend,

Abigail

The Treasurer

MARCH 27, 1614

Dear Elizabeth,

We awoke early, but there was still no sign of John and Robert. They have been gone a full day now. Pocahontas and I were too anxious to speak. We paced the deck and strained to see any sign of them in the distance. Finally, about noon, we rejoiced to see John and Robert return unharmed.

They went directly to the captain's cabin to meet with Deputy Governor Dale and Master Hamor. I wondered if Master Hamor had shown anyone Master Rolfe's letter. The men stayed there for more than two hours.

Pocahontas and I walked the deck of the ship arm in arm. Words were not necessary as we waited for the news. Had her father redeemed her? What was her fate?

Finally, the men came up on deck for a walk. Deputy Governor Dale told us that the mission had gone well. Chief Powhatan, fearing the tricks of the English, would not meet with Master Rolfe and Robert. Instead they met with the chief's brother Opechankano, who is the next in line for chief. He assured them he would use his influence to further our requests.

Pocahontas asked, "So we do not know whether my father will redeem me?"

Deputy Governor Dale replied, "No. But then, your father may have other decisions to make." He smiled as he walked away.

Pocahontas and I looked at each other. What could that mean?

Then Master Rolfe asked if he could escort Pocahontas on a short walk. He was quite formal. Again, Pocahontas and I looked at each other. The men were acting so strangely. Robert told me of his adventure in the company of the Indians, but I was distracted. I much preferred to know what Master Rolfe was saying to Pocahontas. When they returned, Pocahontas was smiling and Master Rolfe winked at Robert.

Master Rolfe said, "I hear I am to thank you, Miss Abigail." I must

have looked perplexed for he continued, "I understand a certain letter I wrote and entrusted to Reverend Whitaker found its way to your care."

"I did not read it, Master Rolfe. But I knew it had to do with your love for Pocahontas."

"A love that would have remained silent if you had not acted as you did. Why did you give the letter to Master Hamor?"

"Robert told me of your noble treatment of Pocahontas and that, despite your feelings for her, you would not tell her until she had made a decision about her faith. What you did not know, Master Rolfe, was that Pocahontas had made a decision to become a Christian. I only learned of it a few nights ago. She too did not want her feelings for you to confuse that important decision. I suspected, knowing your deep faith, and your many hours of secret conversations with Reverend Whitaker, that you were struggling with whether or not you could ask the princess to marry you if she chose not to become a Christian.

"It seemed as though all our lives were about to be changed by a decision made by Deputy Governor Dale. I thought that he should know all the facts if he was about to make an important decision about Pocahontas's fate. I had no idea if Master Hamor would give the letter to Deputy Governor Dale, but since you addressed it to him, I suppose I hoped so."

"Ah, and that is exactly what happened. Deputy Governor Dale is elated with the prospect of a marriage between Pocahontas and myself. But first, of course, I had to know whether Pocahontas would be equally as pleased."

"And?" I asked, looking at Pocahontas.

She leaned on Master Rolfe's arm and said, "John has told me of his love and his desire for marriage. I would like that too, but only if it will help bring about the peace we all so desire. I have asked John to go to my father and ask him if he will bless our marriage. If so, I will be delighted to become Mrs. John Rolfe."

Oh, no, Elizabeth, more *waiting!* I can hardly stand it. What if her father says no? What then?

Your friend,

Abigail

The Treasurer

MARCH 28, 1614

Dear Elizabeth,

Master Rolfe and Robert again went to visit the chief. This time, accompanied by Pocahontas's brothers, he was willing to hear Master Rolfe's request to marry his daughter. Robert told me that Master Rolfe passionately pleaded for the hand of Pocahontas in marriage and promised to honor her all her days. It must have been pleasing to Chief Powhatan because he swiftly gave his approval.

Back on ship, all rejoiced as we set sail for Henricus. I cannot wait to tell Reverend Whitaker. And Mrs. Sizemore! Oh, my goodness, will she ever be pleased. I can see her now, fiddling with every nip and tuck in a wedding dress for the princess.

We are all exhausted, but very, very happy.

Your friend,

Abigail

Rock Hall

March 31, 1614

Dear Elizabeth,

Today Reverend Whitaker baptized Pocahontas into the Christian faith. The baptismal font was filled with fresh spring water. Reverend Whitaker looked splendid in his white robes. Reverend Bucke from James Towne and many others attended.

I was thrilled to see the Pierces again. Jane is growing up fast, a girl of thirteen now. She is quite lovely. She asked that you give her love to Temperance. Temperance was always such a dear to Jane and kept her cheerful during that horrible year with no food.

Princess Pocahontas looked radiant in a white robe. Mrs. Sizemore has been busy with both the baptismal robe and the wedding dress to prepare in less than ten days. The wedding is less than a week away. You cannot imagine the clucking going on at Rock Hall these days!

The baptism service was quite remarkable. Reverend Whitaker presented Pocahontas to those in attendance. She was now ready to make her confession of faith and to receive the baptism. He said that today Pocahontas would receive a new name, the name of Rebecca.

Reverend Whitaker asked Pocahontas—I mean, Rebecca—many questions of the faith. Rebecca renounced the devil and all his works. I could not help but think of the devil god Okee that she had learned to fear—the devil god who demanded child sacrifices. Rebecca spoke the creed in a strong voice, and at the end said, "All this I steadfastly believe."

Reverend Whitaker poured water from the font on her head and said, "I baptize thee in the name of the Father, and of the Son, and of the Holy Ghost. Amen." She looked steadily at Reverend Whitaker, who spoke of what this act of baptism means.

Then we all bowed our heads and prayed the Lord's Prayer. Reverend Whitaker challenged Rebecca that now that she was a child of God and had been baptized, she should walk by the light of faith to be made like Jesus. I have never seen her look more radiant.

Mrs. Sizemore, who was sitting with me, passed me a handkerchief. We both dabbed at our eyes as we realized the incredible miracle that had taken place in Pocahontas's long journey to faith in Jesus. I stole a glance at Master Rolfe, who gazed upon Rebecca, beautiful in her white robe and shining face, with such joy.

That afternoon the streets filled with people. Music filled the air as we celebrated the baptism of Pocahontas. When I asked her what she thought of her new name, she said that Reverend Whitaker had chosen it, but had asked her about his choice. He read her the story in the Bible of Isaac, Abraham's son, and Rebekah and the miracle of how they found each other, each trusting in the will of God for their marriage.

Master Rolfe and Rebecca walked together through the crowd. Soon, they will be married. I could not be happier for my friend and companion, dearest Pocahontas, little Snow Feather, who is now Rebecca, which means in English, "to bind closely to another."

Reverend Whitaker came by and whispered in my ear, "God used you to draw Pocahontas to himself."

I looked at him with surprise.

"Do you remember that day in the garden a few days before the *Treasurer* left? Pocahontas had already made her commitment to Jesus more than a month before. Yet, she was not sure that you would approve. She told me she would not make a public declaration of her faith until she was sure it would not hurt you."

"What?"

"She knew that the loss of your mother and father deeply affected you. She was not sure you could share your heavenly Father with her. She thought that if you found out she had become a Christian, you would resent her and think that she had taken away your heavenly Father as well as your earthly father."

"I would not think that!"

"I know. I tried to tell her this would not be so, but I think,

Abigail, she knew more about your pain than I did. I encouraged her to talk with you about it. When she asked if you could forgive her father, she really wanted to know if you had room in your heart for her to know your heavenly Father and call him her own. She loves you very much and did not want to hurt you."

I was moved by the concern she gave to my heart's pain.

"Then you forgave Chief Powhatan for his role in the death of your parents and you sought Pocahontas's forgiveness for how you had treated her. By that, she knew the power of the forgiveness of Christ in a way she had not understood before. She responded to it completely."

"I had no idea."

"Usually we do not, Abigail. The power of forgiveness, especially forgiveness that comes at great cost, is a power we likely will never fully understand until we get to heaven. The Scriptures tells us that what is bound on earth is bound in heaven and what is loosed on earth is loosed in heaven. We cannot even imagine the power of the grace of God."

I am deeply humbled. I have learned much in this year with Pocahontas. Much about myself and much about my heavenly Father.

Your friend from Rock Hall, the place of new names,

Abigail

James Towne

April 4, 1614

Dear Elizabeth,

Tomorrow is the wedding! Reverend Bucke and Reverend Whitaker will both perform the ceremony at the church here.

Oh, my, have the church ladies been busy. This past week, I have had to rescue Rebecca from Mrs. Sizemore more than once. She managed to gather the finest Dacca muslin, a veil of lace, and a robe of fine English brocade to make Rebecca's wedding dress. Where do you suppose the robe of fine brocade came from? Your father's birthday gift to me of several years ago has finally found its rightful home.

Rebecca and I are staying with the Pierces. Mistress Pierce is such a no-nonsense woman that we find ourselves right at home. Jane adores Rebecca and has been busy picking flowers to decorate the church. Chief Powhatan sent a beautiful freshwater pearl necklace for his daughter to wear.

He will not attend the wedding, but he sent two of Pocahontas's brothers and her uncle Opitchapan. They brought two baskets of dirt, another present from her father. Chief Powhatan is giving his daughter and her husband many acres of valuable land. The baskets of dirt are from that land. Pocahontas's brothers are having a fine time. They brought venison for the wedding feast. Master Rolfe and Robert are making sure they feel welcome. They have even taught them to bowl.

Tonight, it took all of us to get Mrs. Sizemore to leave. The wedding is in the morning so she brought over the wedding dress, the veil, the robe, and the shoes. She does not trust us. She was clucking around quite a bit and seemed reluctant to leave her treasures in our care. Mistress Pierce assured her that Rebecca would be properly dressed and ready long before the ceremony.

After repeated assurances that we would not muss the dress, Mrs. Sizemore finally left.

Mistress Pierce, always thoughtful of others, took Jane to visit the Smythes and left us alone. Rebecca and I laughed as we recalled our many adventures of the past year. I gave my impression of her in her first English corset tied tight around her ribs, and she gave her impression of me learning to ride Admiral.

We have taught each other much this year, but nothing more important than the value of true friendship. On this last night before her wedding, we agreed we will be friends forever. Rebecca asked if she could have one last special favor—to carry my father's Bible during the wedding ceremony. It brought such joy to me to think that she would honor my father in this way.

I wish she had known him, Elizabeth. They would have truly liked each other.

With great joy,

Abigail

James Towne

April 5, 1614

Dear Elizabeth,

It is late now, and quiet in the Pierces' home. I have a few minutes to write to tell you about the wedding. The bells rang this morning at 10:00 a.m. to call everyone to the church. I stayed with Mistress Pierce and Mrs. Sizemore to help Rebecca get ready.

On the second bells, we walked with Rebecca to the church. I lifted the end of her robe to keep it from touching the dirt. Rebecca wore the pearl necklace from her father. She carried my father's Bible with a bouquet of flowers that Jane had gathered for her. She looked so beautiful.

We took her to her uncle Opitchapan, who willingly gave her away. Her brothers stood with him and yet looked tenderly at their sister. They know she is happy now.

Master Rolfe, with Robert by his side, could not take his eyes off his bride as she approached the front of the church. Reverend Whitaker stood at the front of the church too. He was beaming. What a glorious day for all of us.

After they stated their vows and Master Rolfe placed a ring on Rebecca's hand, they took communion. Then Reverend Whitaker prayed, "Look, O Lord, look mercifully upon them from heaven, and bless them. And send thy blessing upon these thy servants; that they, obeying thy will and always being in safety under thy protection, may abide in thy love unto their lives' end; through Jesus Christ our Lord. Amen."

The bells began to ring and continued until everyone had left the church. Mr. and Mrs. John Rolfe were surrounded by many well-wishers. There was much feasting and celebration, for not only was this a marriage of deep and abiding love, there was great hope this would be a marriage for peace.

Watching Rebecca's brothers and uncle enjoying themselves

during the feast made me wonder if this dream might be possible. If anyone could bring peace to this troubled colony, it would be Pocahontas — a girl who always knew her own mind, a strong-spirited, determined girl who for years had dreamed of peace between her people and the English. Perhaps now in this most unusual and unexpected way, there will be peace.

Dear Elizabeth, your father can rest easy now. If anyone can make a go of this colony, it will be John and Rebecca Rolfe, partners in business, and partners of the heart. Robert has asked Reverend Whitaker again if he might court me. Perhaps that is not such a bad idea after all.

Forever your friend,

Abigail

London, England

April 12, 1614

My Dear Abigail,

I have reread all your letters—from the first to the last. You, my dearest friend, discovered more in Virginia than either of us could ever have imagined. You found adventure, yes, but in your adventures, you discovered the power of forgiveness to redeem even the most desperate of situations. You, Abigail Matthews, among all the young women I know, are most blessed.

Your friend,

Elizabeth

Notes on Contractions and Pace of Letters

Writing Style of Elizabeth and Catherine

We are quite comfortable using contractions. Contractions such as *won't*, *haven't*, and *it's* sound familiar; whereas *will not*, *have not*, and *it is* sound formal and a bit stilted. However, that wasn't always the case. Contractions were not used in diaries, journals, or letters in England or the new colony until the mid 17th century, and even then, the only contraction used was *it's* or *'tis*. It wasn't until the 18th century that contractions became more commonplace in both speech and writing.

Pace of Elizabeth and Catherine's Letters

Note the change of pace in the letters between the girls. Early in the book, the letters span many months because few ships sailed between England and its Virginia colony. As England began to supply the colony more frequently, the girls' letters traveled to each other in six to eight weeks instead of six to eight months.

Epilogue

In 1615, Thomas was born to John and Rebecca Rolfe. Chief Powhatan promised that as long as Pocahontas lived, there would be peace.

In 1616, the Virginia Company decided England should meet the American princess, Lady Rebecca. Rebecca traveled to London with her family and her sister Matachanna. Rebecca attended plays, dinners, balls, and pageants. In early 1617, John Rolfe moved his family to the English countryside for a break from the activities and the unhealthy city air of London.

When Rebecca and Thomas fell ill, the Rolfe family set sail for Virginia. Rebecca took a turn for the worse, and they landed at Gravesend for medical help. John carried Rebecca to a cottage near the waterfront. For several days, Rebecca struggled against her illness. Reports noted that she expressed her trust and hope in God and her beloved Savior. She died on March 21, 1617, and was buried the same day in St. George's Parish.

The grieving husband set sail again to Virginia, but Thomas's condition worsened. John Rolfe finally agreed to leave Thomas in the care of his brother rather than risk the loss of his son's life as well. When Thomas was old enough to survive the difficult conditions of Virginia, he would be reunited with his father. Unfortunately, John Rolfe died when Thomas was only six years old. In 1635, when Thomas was twenty years old, he came to Virginia, claimed the land his father had left him, and built a new life in America.

The peace between the Indians and the colonists lasted five years after Pocahontas's death. On Good Friday morning, March 22, 1622, Indians gathered at the homes of colonists who had welcomed them during the Peace of Pocahontas. At a prearranged signal, the Indians killed many men, women, and children. More than a fourth of the colonists in Virginia died in a single day. Of the approximately 900 colonists who did survive the attack, half would be dead within the year from disease.

The Pierces

Captain William Pierce became Lieutenant Governor and Captain of James Towne, and served in one of the early General Assemblies of Virginia. Mistress Pierce remained the champion gardener of the colony. In 1620, three years after Rebecca died, John Rolfe married their daughter, Jane Pierce.

Captain Pierce, his family, and the others who lived in James Towne all survived the March 22, 1622 massacre, thanks to Chanco, an Indian who had become a Christian and lived with Richard Pace. When ordered to kill Captain Pace as part of the planned massacre, Chanco told Captain Pace of the plan. Captain Pace secured his own plantation, rowed across the river, and warned as many people as he could at nearby plantations. He arrived at James Towne just before daylight to warn the colonists there, all of whom survived the attack.

Temperance Flowerdew

Temperance met Captain George Yeardley, one of the *Sea Venture* passengers, before her return from James Towne to London. After another chance meeting with Captain Yeardley in London a few years later, they began to write to each other. In 1619, Temperance returned to Virginia as the wife of Governor George Yeardley.

Governor Yeardley held the first legislative assembly in Virginia and in America from July 30 to August 4, 1619. John Rolfe, secretary and recorder for the colony, attended the Assembly and served as a member of the Governor's Council. Reverend Bucke opened the Assembly in prayer. This first General Assembly addressed the need to establish families in Virginia: "In a new plantation, it is not known whether men or women be more necessary." In 1620, the Virginia Company agreed to send 90 young women to the colony. They very quickly became wives of the colonists.

Reverend Alexander Whitaker

Reverend Whitaker, well respected both in England and America, told his cousin in a letter dated June 18, 1614, that although his three

years of service were over, he would continue to serve the spiritual needs of the colonists. Always close to his heart and ever present on his mind was his stated purpose for coming to Virginia: "That the Gospel may be powerful and effectual by me to the salvation of man and advancement of the Kingdom of Jesus Christ to whom, with the Father and the Holy Spirit, be all honor and glory forevermore."

Elizabeth Walton

Elizabeth never visited Abigail in Virginia. Although not permitted to attend the university herself, she did marry a college graduate from Oxford. She had three daughters and one son. She made sure her daughters were exposed to books of science, medicine, geography, and history, as well as literature. Elizabeth and Abigail continued their correspondence and shared their adventures and their friendship for many years.

Abigail Matthews

Abigail eventually married Robert Sparkes. The first General Assembly in 1619 passed a law requiring each town to commit to the education, both academic and spiritual, of Indian children. The colonists planned to build a school that would prepare children, both Indian and English, for the college planned for Henricus. Because of Abigail's friendship with Pocahontas, several Powhatan parents were willing to let their children come to live with the Sparkes to learn English and to learn about the God of Pocahontas. Many hoped that what began with Pocahontas would continue long after her death. All that changed after the massacre on March 22, 1622, five years and one day after she died. Abigail and Robert, who were visiting the Pierces in James Towne for Good Friday services on that fateful day, escaped the massacre.

The fighting that erupted between the colonists and the Indians as a result saddened Abigail greatly. Abigail Matthews, more than anyone, knew firsthand the power of forgiveness to forge eternal bonds of friendship between the most unlikely of peoples.

Now the Lord is that Spirit:
and where the Spirit of the Lord is, there is liberty.
—2 Corinthians 3:17

Dear Reader,

When I wrote Liberty Letters, I intended to communicate America's journey of freedom and also to illustrate the personal faith journey of girls who made bold choices to help others, and in doing so, helped shape the course of history. Through their stories, we learn the facts, customs, lifestyles of days gone by, and so much more.

The girls I wrote about didn't consider themselves part of "history." Few people do. These were ordinary girls, going about their lives when challenging times occurred in the communities in which they lived. They discovered integrity, courage, hope, and faith within themselves as they met these challenges with creativity and innovation. American history is steeped with just these kinds of people. These people embody liberty.

In *Adventures in Jamestown*, I created the fictional characters of Abigail and Elizabeth as two friends who grew up together but whose lives took very different paths. Abigail's family chose adventure in the New World. Because of that choice, Abigail's life tested her character—sometimes severely—and caused her to look deep within herself for answers about courage, trust, and forgiveness.

Jamestown was founded in 1607, four hundred years ago. Thankfully, archaeologists, through their research, have let us see a little of that time in history. In 1996, they discovered evidence of the actual fort of Jamestown, and then later on, found William Strachey's signet ring.

History books tell us that in 1613, Pocahontas was captured by the colonists, taught the ways of the English, became a Christian, and married John Rolfe. Do you ever wonder what happened to cause her to abandon her Indian heritage, renounce Ahone and Okee (her gods), decide to become a Christian, and then marry John Rolfe? If you look beneath a few lines in a history book, you'll find some great stories!

I did some digging of my own, not for archaeological artifacts, but to learn about Pocahontas, John Rolfe, Alexander Whitaker, and others. I read their letters, sermons, personal writings, and what others who lived during that time wrote about them. Then I asked this question: What if Abigail met Pocahontas? And that's how this story, wrapped in historical events, came about.

Your friend,

Nancy LeSourd

Pocahontas by George Edwards, circa 1910

THE WHITE FIGURE MOVED RAPIDLY

Pocahontas

Matoaka, or Little Snow
Feather, was Pocahontas's
secret tribal name.
Pocahontas was born about
1595 and was the delight of
her father, Chief Powhatan.

John Rolfe

John Rolfe produced a valuable
crop for Virginia. Tobacco,
greatly desired by the English,
was hated by King James I who
called it "hurtful to the health
of the whole body."
John and Pocahantas's marriage
in 1614 and
well-known devotion to each
other established the
"Peace of Pocahontas"
which lasted until 1622.

Susan Constant

The *Susan Constant* was of one of the first ships to arrive at James Towne in 1607. The colonists depended on ships like this one to bring supplies and news from England. An uneventful Atlantic crossing typically took between five and six weeks.

Settlers at James Towne and Henricus

James Towne Street,
English Home, Indian Dwelling

James Towne homes were built of sticks and mud called "wattle and daub" while the English lived in timber-framed houses. Later, the colonists built houses of wood. Powhatan homes, made of mats and bent trees, provided watertight shelter.

Recreated early wattle and daub colonial houses at Jamestown Settlement, Williamsburg, Virginia

English timber-framed home, Hall's Croft. By Permission of the Shakespeare Birthplace Trust

Recreated Powhatan Yehawken at Jamestown Settlement, Williamsburg, Virginia

Pocahontas and Son, Thomas

This portrait of Pocahontas and her son, Thomas, may have been painted from sketches drawn of them while they were visiting John Rolfe's family in England in 1617.

Portrait of Pocahontas and Thomas. Unknown artist, circa 1800. Photo by David Pitcher with permission of Borough Council of King's Lynn and West Norfolk

Regal Pocahontas

The Virginia Company stockholders wanted the English to know Pocahontas ("Lady Rebecca") as the daughter of the "king" of the Powhatans—a royal princess. She looks very English in her features in this painting.

Portrait of Pocahontas by Richard Norris Brooke ca 1905. Virginia Museum of Fine Arts, Richmond. Gift of John Barton Payne. Photo: Ron Jennings. © Virginia Museum of Fine Arts

Hulton Archives-Getty Images

Indian Attack

Colonists, desperate to find food during the Starvation Time, left the protection of the fort to forage for food nearby and were killed by Powhatan arrows.

Burial of the Dead During the Starving Time (Winter 1610) by Sidney King. National Park Service-Colonial National Historical

Burial of the Dead

The colonists buried those who died from starvation at night so they would not alert the Indians to their desperate situation.

The Baptism of Pocahontas

Baptism of Pocahontas at Jamestown, Virginia by John G. Chapman. Located in the Rotunda of the United States Capitol. Courtesy, Architect of the Capitol

"Give thy Holy Spirit to Rebecca; that being born again, and made an heir of everlasting salvation, through our Lord Jesus Christ, she may continue thy servant, and attain thy promises; through the same Lord Jesus Christ thy Son, who liveth and reigneth with thee, and the Holy Spirit, now and forever. Amen"

Book of Common Prayer, 1559

Hornbook

Pocahontas probably learned to read and write using a hornbook like this one.

Secretarie Handwriting

Elizabeth and Abigail wrote to each other using quill pens in the flowing style known as "Secretarie" handwriting.

THE GLOBE THEATRE.

On the Bankside.

As it appeared in the reign of King James I.

Globe Theatre

The Globe Theatre, where many of Shakespeare's plays were performed, burned down in 1613, when a cannon fired during a performance of Henry VIII set fire to a thatched roof.

EMPORIUMQUE TOTO ORBE CELEBERRIMUM.

Philadelphia, Pennsylvania

FOURTH MONTH 27, 1858

Dear Hannah,

I've done it again. This is the third time in as many months that I've brought it up. It was no sooner out of my mouth than I wished I could take it back.

I graduate from Friends Central High in two years, and if I am going to enter Female Medical College, I need to study physiology now. There is so much to learn. And what I really need is a skeleton. So, I asked my parents. Again. For the third time. Big mistake.

Father rambled on about a proper Quaker woman's aspirations. You know, husband, children, home, and service. I reminded him that the Medical College was started by Quakers for Quaker women, and that I could serve by healing others, but he pretended he didn't hear me.

Mother put down her stitching and simply said, "There will be no dead bones in this home."

I promised her Friend Bones (as I like to call him just as I would any other beloved Quaker friend) would be very well behaved. "Friend Bones won't rattle around because I'll hang him from a pole in my room so I can study him better."

Mother tilted her head and began to answer. She stopped short and studied me. It was almost as if she were going to relent, but then, me and my big mouth, I had to fill the silence, didn't I? "Friend Bones," I blurted out, "will be quite at home here. Like one of the family." Mother got up, said she had washing to do, and that was that.

Sometimes I think Father regrets bringing me home from Springdale Boarding School right next door to you and enrolling me at Friends Central High, here in the city. Although Father definitely believes in the equality of all men, regardless of race, I'm not sure he agrees that applies to equality of all men *and women*. Father is not comfortable with the idea of a woman being a doctor.

At the rate I am going, however, it will be a long time before I can become a doctor. Friends Central doesn't offer more-advanced science courses. I guess I shouldn't complain though. Even the boys can't take physiology.

When I'm not pestering my parents about Friend Bones, we spend more and more time working together on getting delivery packages safely to their destinations. Yet, it's more dangerous now than ever to be in the delivery business. And complicated. There are many who would see us fail. The stakes are much higher now — with grave penalties. Ask your grandfather to explain. I should close for now.

Your friend,

Sarah

Goose Creek, Virginia

Sixth Month 2, 1858

Dear Sarah,

I helped Grandfather survey another road today. His map of Loudoun County has been well received and he wants to get this next map published soon. I hope so, because he might take me with him to visit his publisher in Philadelphia … and you!

Joshua came along again to help. He's seventeen and is Uncle Richard's apprentice at the foundry. Although he is only a year older than I am, our lives are so different. He's been an orphan for twelve years now, and ever since, he has had to work to earn his food and lodging.

As usual, I kept the notebook and carefully wrote down everything Grandfather called out to me as he and Joshua worked the chain and compass to measure the road. Joshua and Grandfather can make calculations in their heads faster than I can write them down.

I waited for my chance. When Joshua started to roll up the surveying chain, I showed Grandfather your letter. He read it quickly, then glanced at Joshua, and whispered that I was not to say a word about this to anyone. On the way home, Joshua tried to make me laugh, but my mind was too preoccupied with questions. What is this delivery business that you're involved in? Why is Grandfather being so mysterious? Why won't he talk about it with Joshua around?

After supper, Grandfather asked me to come to the barn with him to brush down Frank. You remember Frank, don't you? Such a solid horse, deserving of such a solid name. Grandfather brushed away some of the hay in Frank's stall and showed me a trapdoor.

Grandfather did not say a word. He just let me look inside with my lamp. I saw a bed of straw and a blanket. I stared inside for a long time. Then Grandfather lowered the trapdoor and spread the hay over it again. Frank nuzzled me, but I could not move. I shivered in the night air even though it was quite warm. Thoughts, questions whirled around in my head.

Grandfather put his hands on my shoulders and said, "The Lord said he came to proclaim liberty to the captives—to set free those in bondage. How can we do any less?" He glanced over his shoulder and continued, "It is fourteen miles from our home to the Potomac River. Once a slave crosses that river, it is but a short journey through Maryland to Pennsylvania ... and freedom."

We walked back to the house in silence. Then I lit my candle stub and came straight to my room to write this letter. I know many of our faith are part of what they call the Underground Railroad, but Grandfather? Sarah, is your family part of this Underground Railroad too? Are these the packages you spoke about? Why are you in danger? Don't you live in a free state? How long has Grandfather been hiding slaves right here at Evergreen? Are we in danger too? I have so many questions. I cannot sleep.

Your friend,
Hannah

Philadelphia, Pennsylvania

Sixth Month 14, 1858

Dear Hannah,

I shared your letter with Mother. She says we must not speak of such things by letter, especially by any letter posted in Virginia. She has a plan, though. Your grandfather arrives tomorrow. I'll send a special present back with him for you.

I have worked my fingers to the bone sewing all week. We need shirts, lots of shirts. I'll explain more later. Hannah, I'm afraid that our friendship quilt must wait a bit longer. There is not time right now to work on it.

I had a brilliant idea to win Father over about Friend Bones. I think he's worried I want to live in a man's world and am not dedicated to becoming a proper Quaker woman. So, today I rode the horse-drawn omnibus to Forty-Fourth and Haverford to volunteer at the Association for the Care of Colored Orphans. Right now there are 67 boys and girls, from babies to nine year olds, living at the Shelter.

I asked the director if I could help with nursing the children when they are sick. Sounds noble, but I figured that with this many children here, the doctor is likely to stop by often. So, maybe I could learn medicine while I help out. Mrs. Whitaker said right now she needs my help to tutor the older children in reading, writing, and basic computations.

Mrs. Whitaker told me about a new boy who arrived last week. He's seven years old, and his name is Zebulon Coleman. I glanced in his direction. "He seems scared," I commented.

Mrs. Whitaker nodded. "The children are often frightened when they first arrive. New surroundings. New people." She lowered her voice to a whisper. "Something terrible happened to Zebulon's parents, so he may need more time to adjust."

I started to ask her what happened, but she turned and walked over to Zebulon to introduce him to me.

Zebulon didn't speak when I greeted him. He lowered his eyes and stared at the same spot on the floor. I tried my best to let him know I was friendly, but his eyes didn't budge.

I wonder what happened to Zebulon's family.

On the way out, I bumped into a man with a suitcase. He tipped his hat and said, "Peter Pennington, at your service."

I said hello but felt uneasy.

He continued, "New girl, eh? Going to help out?"

I brushed past him without an answer. How did he know who I was? What business is it of his anyway? Who is this man? I hope he isn't staying here.

Your friend,

Sarah

Goose Creek, Virginia

SIXTH MONTH 25, 1858

Dear Sarah,

As soon as Grandfather arrived home, I asked about my present from you. He smiled and handed me a little seedling in a big clay pot. Not exactly what I was expecting from my best friend. You know I can get tree seedlings from Grandfather's nursery any time I want.

After a few moments he said, "Hannah, thee is so disappointed! Come with me. There is more to this little seedling than meets the eye."

Grandfather led me to a table in the greenhouse and turned the pot upside down. All the dirt not attached to the roots rolled out onto the table, as did a small leather pouch. Inside were your letters!

What a magnificent idea your mother had to hide your letters in a pot. Now when I write back, Grandfather will carry my letters to you the same way. It's just another pot with other cuttings from our nursery here at Evergreen to sell in Philadelphia. No one will ever guess our secret. If we must speak about things better left unspoken, this will do quite nicely.

Grandfather had another surprise for me. A buyer for the cuttings from the Ginko tree did not have enough cash to make the purchase. Instead, he opened a velvet pouch of pearls and other gems. Grandfather selected a perfect, milky white pearl in payment. He said that when he saw it, he thought of me and wanted me to have this as a token of his love for me.

Have you worked on our friendship quilt lately? I will take my leather pouch to bed tonight and read your letters by candlelight.

Your friend,
Hannah

Richmond, Virginia

JUNE 17, 1861

Dear Emma,

I couldn't believe my eyes. "Private Franklin Thompson, of the Second Michigan Volunteers," you said. "Requesting donations for the Union Army, ma'am."

While Great Auntie Belle scurried around, loading my arms with linens, food, and medicines, so many questions swirled around in my head. How did you get to Michigan? And what, pray tell, possessed you to enlist in the Union Army? As you carried the supplies outside to the ambulance, I barely heard you whisper, "You'll keep my secret, won't you?"

"Such a nice young man, Mollie," Great Auntie commented, arms filled with more donations.

Young man? This is no man—this is Emma! I thought. *Emma, my good friend.* Last summer I was shocked when you confided in me that you left Canada with your mother's blessing to escape your cruel father. You even fooled everyone in New England, selling books disguised as a boy—one of Mr. Hurlburt's finest door-to-door salesmen. But this? A soldier in the war? Really, Emma! You've gone too far!

Your friend,

Mollie

Washington, D.C.

JUNE 22, 1861

Dear Mollie,

I know I need to explain. When Mr. Hurlburt offered me the chance to work in Flint, Michigan, I jumped at the chance to see more of this adopted country of mine. Mollie, I had to keep up my disguise. After all, I had to make a living.

Then I heard the newsboy cry out, "Fall of Fort Sumter —President's Proclamation—Call for 75,000 men!" It's true I'm not an American. When President Lincoln called for men to fight for my adopted country, I couldn't turn away. I had to help free the slaves. After much prayer, I knew God meant for me to enlist in the Army. So when my friends volunteered for the Second Regiment of the Michigan Volunteer Infantry, I assumed God would make a way for me too. But I missed the height requirement by two inches.

The day my friends left, the people of Flint cheered them on. The boys lined up with their bright bayonets flashing in the morning sunlight. Almost every family had a father, husband, son, or brother in that band of soldiers. The pastor preached a sermon and presented a New Testament to each one. Then as the bands played the "Star-Spangled Banner," the soldiers marched off to Washington. Oh, how I wanted to be with them!

A few weeks later, who should return to Flint, but my old friend from church, William Morse, now *Captain* William Morse who came back to recruit more soldiers for his regiment. This time I was ready. I stuffed my shoes with paper and stood as tall as I could. It worked! I was now Private Franklin Thompson of Company F of the Second Michigan Volunteer Infantry of the United States Army.

When I got to Washington, the army assigned me to be a field nurse. All the field nurses are men, and it doesn't matter if you don't have any training as a nurse. They tell us we'll learn it all from the field surgeons as we go. I reported to the Surgeon in charge and received my first order to visit the temporary hospitals set up all over the city. Although there are no battle injuries yet, many are sick with typhoid and malaria. There are not enough beds for the sick; not enough doctors to treat them; and not enough medicines and food.

That's why some of us decided to visit the good ladies of Washington and plead with them to donate to the Union. That was the day I saw you again—a most fortunate day for me. I hope you feel the same.

Your friend,
Private Frank Thompson, Company F,
Second Michigan Regiment
(Emma)

Richmond, Virginia

JUNE 28, 1861

Dear Emma,

Of course, I was glad to see you again, but just how do you think you can pull this off—being a private in the United States Army? Sure you can handle nursing duties. But what about shooting and riding a horse, marching and drilling, standing guard and picket duty? Can you keep your secret much longer?

Great Auntie has arranged for our letters to get to each other through her private courier now that the federal government has suspended mail to the Southern states. She is delighted I want to write to a Federal soldier. I'll address your letters to Frank so there is no suspicion. Is it all right to call you Emma in the letter? I don't want to give you away.

Great Auntie makes no secret of her support of the North, as you saw from her willingness to part with supplies for the Union. To the great embarrassment of my Richmond kin, Great Uncle Chester is now a surgeon with the Union Army and Great Auntie Belle is an outspoken supporter of President Lincoln. If Daddy were still alive, I'm sure he would agree. At least that's what I think. Momma seems to think differently.

When Momma and I arrived at Mrs. Whitfield's home today to sew uniforms for the soldiers, we heard angry voices before we even entered the room. Mrs. Whitfield told the ladies she had personally delivered a handwritten invitation to Miss Elizabeth Van Lew and her mother to join us to sew for the Confederate soldiers, but the Van Lews refused to come.

"Let's not forget they sent their daughter, Betty, to that Quaker school in Philadelphia," an outraged Mrs. Morris reminded everyone. "They filled that child's head with abolition talk, and it changed her forever."

"That they did," Mrs. Forrest agreed. "And when Mr. Van Lew died, Betty talked her mother into freeing all their slaves."

Aunt Lydia added, "I heard they even sent one of their slave girls up north to Philadelphia for her schooling and paid for it all!"

I watched the ladies ram their needles through the flannel shirts they were stitching with as much force as the words they were speaking. Personally, I think these ladies are petty gossips. So what if Miss Van Lew believes what the Union does? Is that a crime? It seems so. If they only knew what I believed, they would not permit me in their company. A Southern girl with Northern thoughts. I kept my head down as these ladies spoke. I didn't want them to see the fire in my eyes.

I excused myself as soon as I could and slipped out without much notice. No one pays much attention to a sixteen-year-old girl these days. The women worry about their boys and men and speak endlessly of the impending battles. Their attention is not on the comings and goings of someone like me.

I took this package to the place the courier designated to drop off our letters. I may have knitted for the Confederates today, but this pair of socks is included for you, my adventurous Union friend. Perhaps they will keep your feet from blistering on those long marches.

Your friend,

Mollie

Washington, D.C.

JULY 1, 1861

Dear Mollie,

Thanks for thinking about how to protect my secret. To tell the truth, I like reading my name again. To these men, I am just Frank, but to you, my good friend, I am Emma. I keep your letters tucked inside my shirt so no one can read them. I suppose for now, though, you should continue to address your letters to Frank, but just call me E in the letter. If I should lose a letter, I don't want to risk being found out.

As for riding a horse or shooting a gun, what do you think I did all those years when I was growing up on our farm in New Brunswick, Canada? I can outride and outshoot most anyone — thank you, Miss Mollie. If God has called me to this, then he has prepared me and equipped me to do what I must do. Farming was no harder work. Just try chopping and clearing the land some time, Mollie. Why, you should have seen me swing my ax to hew beams from timber as fast as the next boy. No sirree, if I'm found out, it will not be because I failed to hold my own with these brave men.

Washington is overrun with soldiers. White tents dot the landscape all around the city. The Capitol and the White House shelter hundreds of soldiers, who sit around playing cards and wait for action. Thousands of soldiers drill in the streets. Blasts from bugles and the rat-tat-tat of drums fill the air. All are eager to fight. The rebellion should be put down quickly.

Your friend,

Emma

Richmond, Virginia

JULY 4, 1861

Dear Emma,

Richmond celebrated Independence Day today, but I had to wonder, is it independence from England years ago or independence from the North it celebrates? Sissy asked me to go with her today to the camps outside the city to watch the soldiers drill. She may be two years older than I, but she has such romantic notions about this war. She thinks she can send her Lemuel off to war and he will return to her a hero. Our friends ride out to the camps every day. They dress up, bring their picnic foods, and wait for the drills to end so they can socialize with the soldiers. It all seems so silly to me—this partying with soldiers. Soldiers and girls alike think we will simply wallop the North in one big battle, and then it'll all be over. I'm not so sure.

I don't agree with you that this will be a short war. You think the boys in blue will crush the boys in gray. But here in Richmond, we too have white tents dotting the landscape like snow. Our soldiers march day and night, eager to meet the enemy. We too have hundreds, if not thousands, of young men who are certain we will capture Washington and take over the White House and Capitol where your soldiers now lounge. I do not think victory will come so easily, my dear friend, not to either side.

As the South Carolina regiment marched past us, the girls waved their handkerchiefs and cheered. They debated which regiment is the most handsome. The general consensus of our friends is that the boys from South Carolina are definitely the best looking, although the Texas regiment is a close runner-up with their rugged good looks. You see how deep their thoughts go about this war, Emma. Skin deep.

My attention was on two women handing out food and flowers to the South Carolinians. A murmur spread through the crowd. It was Miss Van Lew and her mother who smiled as they handed out their gifts.

Liberty Letters

Escape on the Underground Railroad
Softcover • ISBN 9780310713913

Together, two girls living a world apart must outwit slave catchers
and assist a runaway South Carolina slave girl on her perilous trip
from Virginia to Canada on the Underground Railroad. Excellent for
educators and homeschool use.

Liberty Letters

Attack at Pearl Harbor
Softcover • ISBN 9780310713890

Determined to learn to fly, Meredith experiences consequences that
will unwittingly provide her just what she needs when the Japanese
bomb Pearl Harbor in 1941, and her best friend's determination to
report on unfolding events puts her family right in the center of the
story. Excellent for educators and homeschool use.

Available now at your local bookstore!